W9-ACI-776

Also by M. C. Beaton

AGATHA RAISIN

Dishing the Dirt

The Blood of an Englishman

Something Borrowed, Someone Dead

Hiss and Hers

As the Pig Turns

Busy Body

There Goes the Bride

A Spoonful of Poison

Kissing Christmas Goodbye

Love, Lies and Liquor

The Perfect Paragon

The Deadly Dance

Agatha Raisin and the Haunted House

Agatha Raisin and the Case of the Curious Curate

Agatha Raisin and the Day the Floods Came

Agatha Raisin and the Love from Hell

Agatha Raisin and the Fairies of Fryfram

Agatha Raisin and the Witch of Wyckhadden

Agatha Raisin and the Wizard of Evesham

Agatha Raisin and the Wellspring of Death

Agatha Raisin and the Terrible Tourist

Agatha Raisin and the Murderous Marriage

The Walkers of Dembley

The Potted Gardener

The Vicious Vet

The Quiche of Death

The Skeleton in the Closet

EDWARDIAN MYSTERY SERIES

Our Lady of Pain

Sick of Shadows

Hasty Death

Snobbery with Violence

Pushing Up Daisies

An Agatha Raisin Mystery

M. C. BEATON

St. Martin's Paperbacks

This is a work of fiction. All of the characters, organizations, and events portrayed in this novel are either products of the author's imagination or are used fictitiously.

PUSHING UP DAISIES

For information address St. Martin's Press, 175 Fifth Avenue, New York, N.Y. 10010.

ISBN: 978-1-250-05745-7

Our books may be purchased in bulk for promotional, educational, or business use. Please contact your local bookseller or the Macmillan Corporate and Premium Sales Department at (800)-221-7945, extension 5442, or by e-mail at MacmillanSpecialMarkets@macmillan.com.

Printed in the United States of America

Minotaur hardcover edition / September 2016
St. Martin's Paperbacks edition / August 2017

St. Martin's Paperbacks are published by St. Martin's Press, 175 Fifth Avenue, New York, N.Y. 10010.

10 9 8 7 6 5 4 3 2 1

This book is dedicated to all the Tapping family: Dave, Zoe, Rachael, Hannah, and last, but not least, Harry.

With affection

Chapter One

Agatha Raisin, private detective, resident in the Cotswold village of Carsely, should have been a contented and happy woman. Business at her agency was brisk. It was a rare fine English autumn. But the serpent of jealousy was hissing in her ear. Agatha had been jealous of women before, but never in one hundred years had she expected to be jealous of her best friend, Mrs. Bloxby, the vicar's wife.

There was a newcomer in the village, Gerald Devere, a retired New Scotland Yard detective and, of all people, Mrs. Bloxby appeared smitten. She had dyed her hair a rich brown and had taken to wearing attractive clothes instead of her usual old droopy ones.

Gerald was in his early fifties. He had a slim athletic body, a clever mobile face, fine grey eyes and odd slanting black eyebrows. Agatha was determined to ensnare him. After all, she was unmarried, and Mrs. Bloxby was married to the vicar. I will only be doing her a favour, thought Agatha. She surely does not want to break up her marriage.

But Gerald had caught Agatha snooping around his house and had been furious with her. Hard work ahead, getting him to even like me, thought Agatha.

Agatha phoned her friend, Detective Sergeant Bill Wong, and said, "There's a newcomer in Carsely. Says he's a retired New Scotland Yard detective. Know anything about him?"

"Yes. He was a detective inspector with an impeccable record. He could have risen higher, but he decided to retire. Afraid of the competition?"

"Don't need to be," said Agatha. "All my work is in Mircester now. Big town stuff. No village mayhem."

It was a sunny Sunday morning. Agatha felt restless. She had thought about going to church but held back, knowing the sight of Mrs. Bloxby, all dressed up and glowing, might drive her to saying something that could end their valuable friendship.

Then she remembered that Mrs. Bloxby had asked

her aid in helping the people who had allotments outside the village. Their half acres of land were under threat. The land had belonged to a trust but was now owned by Lord Bellington, who wanted to sell it to a developer for a housing estate. Allotments had started in the nineteenth century when the Victorians considered them a good way for the poor to grow their own vegetables. Gradually over the years, their popularity declined, until they suddenly became popular again but with a surprising number of members of the middle class.

Agatha switched on her computer and looked up Lord Bellington. He was a baron. And there's a name to conjure with, thought Agatha. Barons in fairy stories are always wicked. His home and estates lay outside Mircester. She decided to go and talk to him and see if she could persuade him to leave the allotments alone. Agatha fought down a little frisson of fear, remembering during her last case when she had been nearly buried alive in an allotment. But the fact that Mrs. Bloxby might have asked Gerald for help stiffened her spine. She would show him what a private detective could do.

"You are amazing, Agatha," he said over a candlelit supper. He reached forward to take her hand.

The ringing of the doorbell jerked her out of her dream. She found her friend, Sir Charles Fraith, standing on the doorstep. "I was just about to go out," said Agatha.

He followed her in. Although Charles was wearing casual clothes—open-necked blue shirt and dark blue chinos—from his barbered fair hair to his polished shoes, he looked as impeccable as ever.

"You're all made-up and dressed up," said Charles surveying her. "That's your man-hunting appearance. If it's to do with Gerald Devere, forget it. I've already told you not to stamp on Mrs. Bloxby's dreams because she is a good woman and dreams are all they are going to be."

"Well, you're wrong," said Agatha. "I am doing Mrs. Bloxby a favour. The village allotments are under threat."

"Oh, wicked Lord Bellington."

"Do you know him, Charles?"

"Met him here and there."

"I'm off to see if I can melt his heart."

"I'll come with you," said Charles. "He doesn't have a heart. He has a swinging brick."

Lord Bellington's home, Harby Hall, lay a few miles outside Mircester. It seemed to be well guarded. First, they were challenged at the entrance lodge before they were let into the drive. Further up the drive, they were flagged down by a gamekeeper who also demanded

their business. "Just visiting," said Charles, the expla-
nation he had given the lodge keeper.

They drove on until they came to the mansion. "It's
actually uglier than mine," said Charles.

It was a turreted monstrosity, built by some Victorian during the craze for mediaeval architecture. The
windows were small and diamond paned. The front
was dominated by a large portico. They approached
a massive oak door studded with brass.

Charles rang the bell. The door was opened by a
young woman wearing a bikini. She had a round white
face and very small black eyes. Her black hair was wet.
Her brief bikini displayed rolls of white fat, and her
legs were covered in black hairs.

"What do you want?" she demanded.

"We wish to speak to Lord Bellington," said
Charles.

"Dad's in the pool. Does he know you?"

"Yes," said Charles.

"Okay. Follow me."

The entrance hall was very dark and lined with suits
of armour. Tattered battle flags hung from the ceiling.
The girl trotted in front of them, dripping water. She
led the way through a door at the back of the hall,
down stone steps, along a corridor and so into a large
humid room with a large swimming pool.

A large hairy man, absolutely naked, was sitting in a chair by the pool, drying his feet with a towel.

"Friends of yours, Dad," said his daughter and plunged into the pool.

He had a pugnacious face and suspicious little eyes peering out below thick shaggy eyebrows. "Don't know you," he said.

"I'm Charles Fraith. Met you last year at the hunt ball."

"Oh, that's who you are. This your wife?"

"No. May I introduce Agatha Raisin?"

Now he's drying his crotch, thought Agatha. If only he would put some clothes on.

"Come upstairs and we'll have a drink." Lord Bellington heaved himself to his feet and, to Agatha's relief, shrugged himself into a large dressing gown.

They followed him back upstairs and through to a room on the ground floor. "This is my study," he said, opening a drinks cupboard. "What's your poison?"

Agatha asked for a gin and tonic and Charles, whisky and soda. The room was cluttered with hunting boots, game bags and fishing rods. A large salmon in a glass case eyed them mournfully. A stuffed fox on a side table snarled as if it wanted to leap forward and take a bite out of them. Thick ivy outside the window sent flutters of sunlight into the room.

Charles and Agatha sat side by side on a battered

sofa that creaked alarmingly. Lord Bellington sat behind an ornately carved desk, took a large swig of some purplish drink and asked, "Why have you come?"

"It's about the allotments in Carsely," said Agatha. "If you build those houses, it means Carsely could lose village status and become a town. There are already two people in the village who have been trying for years to build housing estates, and now they will feel they can do it."

"Do you think I give a damn about what a lot of pesky villagers want?" he demanded.

"Do you need the money?" asked Charles.

"You should know that estates bleed money. You can tell those creeps in Carsely they haven't a hope in hell of making me change my mind."

"Who inherits if you die?" asked Agatha.

"Thinking of bumping me off? My son, Damian, inherits. Although he's such a weakling, I'm thinking of changing my will. Now, bugger off. I want my lunch."

"And that's that," said Charles. "We'll tell Mrs. Bloxby we at least tried."

"I haven't had breakfast," said Agatha. "What about stopping at some greasy spoon and getting the full English?"

"Good idea."

But when they arrived at the vicarage, it was to find the drawing room full of people. "It is a meeting to discuss the allotments," said Mrs. Bloxby. She was wearing a pink sheath dress and black patent court shoes. Her face was made-up, and her hair had been cut in a fashionable crop, making her look younger. Gerald Devere seemed to be in charge of the meeting.

Agatha smiled at him and then said in a loud voice, "I am afraid we have bad news. We have been to see Lord Bellington, and he is not going to budge an inch."

To her fury, Gerald said, "You should have consulted us first. Someone more diplomatic might have fared better."

"I know Bellington," said Charles. "And nothing short of bumping him off is going to solve the problem."

"Well, I'm going to see him," said a tall, rangy woman. Agatha recognised her as being a Miss Bunty Daventry. "I'll talk to him man-to-man. Straight from the shoulder."

"I'll come with you," said her friend. What was her name again? Agatha suddenly remembered. Josephine Merriweather, a small restless woman with a face like an outraged ferret.

"Do your best," said Agatha, "but I assure you, it's hopeless."

"Why don't we let Mr. Devere be our emissary?" suggested Mrs. Bloxby. "I mean, as an ex-Scotland Yard detective, he must be good at dealing with difficult people. Let's have a vote."

The majority voted that Gerald should go. The allotment holders were a mixture of middle-class ladies and crusty old men. One of the old men, Harry Perry, said, "I won first prize two years running with me marrow. He can't take fame like that away from me."

Agatha hated not being in control. "Listen!" she said. "I'll get in touch with the local newspapers and drum up support."

"Now that is a good idea," said Gerald and smiled at Agatha for the first time. The glow on Mrs. Bloxby's face dimmed like the shadow of a cloud passing over a field.

As the meeting started to break up, Gerald asked Charles for directions to Lord Bellington's place. Mrs. Bloxby whispered to Agatha, "Stay behind."

Oh, dear, thought Agatha. Is she going to talk about Gerald?

But when only Charles and Agatha were left, Mrs. Bloxby said, "I am very worried. Feelings are running high."

"I suppose that's understandable," said Charles. "When Bellington goes ahead with the houses, they'll lose their plots of land."

"It's not that," said the vicar's wife. "Someone has been thieving vegetables from the plots, and tempers are getting out of hand. Miss Merriweather reported the thefts to the police, and they refused to have anything to do with it, so Miss Merriweather is going around saying if she got her hands on the thief, she would kill him."

"Could be a she," said Agatha.

"In Miss Merriweather's opinion, women are beyond reproach," said Mrs. Bloxby.

The vicar, Alf Bloxby, came in. "Just going over to Winter Parva," he said. He turned to go and then swung round and surveyed his wife with a puzzled look. "Are we going anywhere special this evening because I've got evensong at Ancombe?"

"No, dear."

"But you're all dressed up and your hair is different!"

Spare us, thought Agatha. He's just noticed.

"I felt like a change," said his wife. "Do run along. You'll be late."

When the vicar had gone, Charles said, "You do look very well these days."

"Thank you," said Mrs. Bloxby.

Charles sensed that Agatha was on the point of saying something that she certainly should not. "Come along," he said. "I'm sure Mrs. Bloxby has a lot of parish duties to attend to."

Outside Charles rounded on Agatha. "If you say one thing about her crush on Gerald, it's an end to our friendship."

"But she'll get hurt!"

"She's not a child and it is none of your business. You want him for yourself."

"Don't be silly."

"I do wish you would grow up, Aggie. Always chasing after the unattainable like some spotty teenager."

They stood glaring at each other. Then Charles laughed. "Come on. Let's have a drink and maybe stroll down to these pesky allotments."

"You shouted at me," said Agatha in a small voice.

"Trying to get through to you. Let's go to the pub. I hope this Indian summer lasts a bit longer. That is, if one can still call it an Indian summer, or must we now say, 'Native American summer'?"

"Who knows? Who cares?" muttered Agatha, who had not quite forgiven him.

But by the time they drove along to the allotments, Agatha had been restored to good humour and had decided to leave Gerald alone and not interfere in Mrs. Bloxby's life. She felt quite saintly.

The allotments were situated past the council houses outside the village. "They sell their stuff in the village shop," said Charles. "I often buy vegetables to take home."

Agatha wondered if it were possible to cook vegetables in the microwave.

Some people were working their plots, others sat outside small sheds, basking in the sun. "What a lot there is," marvelled Charles. "Pumpkins, leeks, beet-root, carrots and even still some tomatoes."

One allotment was being newly worked by an attractive female turning over the earth with a rotavator. She was wearing a gingham blouse and tight blue jeans. Her long blond hair was tied back with a gingham ribbon. She had a high cheekboned face and large grey eyes.

She saw them watching her and switched off the rotavator. "I wish I could get a gardener in to help me with this," she said. "But the fanatics around here would accuse me of cheating. Hi. I'm Peta Currie, new to the village. You're Agatha Raisin. I've seen your photo in the papers."

"I'm Charles Fraith." Charles shook her hand.

This is heavy competition, thought Agatha. "Won't your husband help you?" she asked.

"Don't have one. Free as the air." She smiled at Charles, who smiled back.

"Which is your cottage?" asked Agatha.

"That one that belonged to that murdered therapist. If you want a reasonably priced cottage in the Cotswolds, go for one that had a murdered body in it."

Agatha felt a stab of fear. She had solved the murder of therapist Jill Davent, only to be nearly murdered herself.

"Better get back to work," said Peta.

Charles and Agatha continued their walk amongst the plots of land. "I remember Mrs. Bloxby telling me they only pay three pounds a year for each half acre. The price was set in World War One. I don't know that I can be bothered finding out who is stealing vegetables," said Agatha. "I've got a lot of work at the moment. And it seems there is nothing more anyone can do about Lord Bellington, may his socks rot."

But as Agatha looked around the peaceful scene, she felt that somehow her dream of peaceful retirement in the Cotswolds had gone wrong. Perhaps she should give up the detective agency and take up gardening instead.

Charles announced he was heading home and dropped Agatha back at her cottage. She wondered how Gerald had fared with Lord Bellington. Probably wouldn't get past the lodge if he were honest about his business, she thought. Perhaps she should call on him and ask him. But she put that idea firmly out of her mind. Charles had made her feel silly.

By evening, she began to feel lonely. Her two cats, Hodge and Boswell, were playing in the garden, seemingly oblivious to her presence. What stupid names for cats. It had all been her ex-husband, James Lacey's, idea.

She scrabbled in her deep freeze, looking for something to microwave. It all looked so unappetising. She decided to go to the pub for dinner.

Agatha regretted her decision as soon as she walked in the doors of the pub. For sitting at a corner table and deep in conversation were Gerald and Peta Currie. Agatha ordered fish and chips and said she would eat her meal in the garden.

Where had Peta come from, wondered Agatha? What was her background? She looked like a model. If Gerald had fallen for Peta, at least Mrs. Bloxby would be safe.

"Wasn't that our village sleuth?" asked Peta.

"Agatha Raisin. Yes," said Gerald.

"Looks quite ferocious."

"I don't like private detectives," said Gerald. "Let's talk about something else."

He was still furious after his interview with Lord Bellington. He had been curtly told to mind his own business and not poke his nose into other people's affairs. A long career of having been treated with respect had made this new brush with the real world infuriating.

He half listened to Peta prattling on about some film she had seen and suddenly wished he could discuss Lord Bellington with Agatha.

Lord Bellington had endured what he considered one awful day. Apart from those interfering people from Carsely, his son Damian had called. Looking more wimpish than ever, and so his father had told him. His daughter, Andrea, looked like frump, and he had told her to go on a diet because she looked sickening. He damned his ex-wife for having divorced him and left him with such awful children. The day before, his mistress, Jenny Coulter, had walked out on him, calling him a bully and a boor.

He ate a large dinner that evening, washed down with a bottle of Sauternes. He had a weakness for sweet wine and always drank a bottle when not in company. He finished his meal with a glass of crème de menthe and decided to have an early night. He suddenly felt drunk. As he climbed into bed, his body was racked with spasms, and he vomited over the place. He bellowed for help, but his son had taken himself back off to London and his daughter had gone to a disco. His housekeeper lived on a cottage on the estate and his chauffeur in a flat above the garage. Nobody heard him, and he doubled up in agony before losing consciousness.

Agatha only heard the news a few days later when his obituary was in the *Times* newspaper. Two weeks later, on a Sunday, she attended a meeting of the allotment users at the vicarage. They were all celebrating. Lord Bellington's heir, his son, Damian, had said he had no intention of building houses on the allotments.

When the cheers had died down, Agatha asked, "How did he die?"

"Vomiting and seizure followed by heart and kidney failure," said Gerald, who had heard the news from police contacts.

"Really? Sounds like classic antifreeze poisoning," said Agatha.

They all stared at her. Then Peta began to laugh. "Haven't you enough to do at that agency of yours without inventing murders?"

"I watch a lot of real-life crime on television," said Agatha huffily. "It would amaze you the number of people bumped off with antifreeze, and it is always diagnosed at first as heart failure."

But the cheerful conversation resumed. Only Gerald suddenly felt uneasy. He had made friends at Mircester police headquarters. Inspector Wilkes had been acidulous on the subject of Agatha, but Detective Sergeant Bill Wong had said that at times Agatha's intuition had been uncanny.

He quietly left the room and went home to make phone calls. As a result of his calls, Damian was asked if his father could possibly have been poisoned. Damian had shrugged and then had said airily, "He's in the family vault. Have a look if you want."

The following Sunday, just as Agatha was gloomily feeding a frozen curry into the microwave, her doorbell rang. She wondered if it could possibly be James

Lacey or Charles but to her surprise, it was Gerald, saying, "May I come in?"

"Yes," said Agatha, wishing she weren't wearing a cotton skirt, t-shirt and flat sandals.

She led the way into her sitting room and offered him a drink. He asked for a whisky and soda. Agatha poured him one, got herself a gin and tonic and asked, "What's the reason for the visit?"

"You were right," said Gerald. "I've just heard. Lord Bellington was poisoned with antifreeze. I'm to take you in to headquarters to make a statement."

"How did you find out?"

"I was worried about what you said. I made phone calls. The son said that as his father was in a stone coffin in the family vault, we could take a look if we wanted and signed the necessary papers. As both of us saw him on the last day of his life, the police want to interview us."

"I hate this," said Agatha. "Wilkes will treat me as if I am the murderer and keep me half the night."

Wilkes was furious with Agatha. He found it hard to believe that she could suspect antifreeze poisoning when she had not even seen the dead body. Therefore, she must have had something to do with the death. After all, she had been in his home. Agatha pointed out that Gerald Devere had been there as well and also she had been accompanied by Charles. She explained that she watched a lot of real-life crime on television and was always amazed at the amount of deaths from antifreeze that went undiagnosed until some wife or husband bumped off the next spouse. At last, the long interview was over and to her fury, she heard herself being told not to leave the country.

Gerald was waiting for her when she left. "Rotten time?" he asked.

"Wilkes is a fool!" raged Agatha.

"He feels you made him look stupid," said Gerald. He ran her to her cottage but refused her offer of a drink.

Which was just as well, thought Agatha sourly, when she walked into her sitting room to find Charles asleep on the sofa with the cats on his lap. She shook him awake.

"Bellington was poisoned," said Agatha, "and as I was the one who suggested it, Wilkes is determined to make me prime suspect. Why weren't you interviewed as well?"

"Have been," said Charles lazily. "That nice detective, Alice Peterson, was sent over to my home."

"It's enough to make anyone a Communist," said Agatha. "Such as you gets the kid-glove treatment while proles like me are dragged in and told not to leave the country."

"Sit down. Calm down. Let's talk about it. It can't have been the son, surely, or he would not have agreed so easily to his father's body being taken out of the vault for another autopsy. Could be the daughter. Or do you think one of the people from the allotments went there and spiked his booze?"

"Can't be. They'll have checked with that lodge keeper who visited him. Wait a bit," said Agatha, shoving Charles's legs onto the floor and sitting down next to him, oblivious of her cats' complaints at being disturbed. "The antifreeze must have been in something he drank. Someone could have doctored a bottle of wine and just waited. Does he have any staff?"

"He has a housekeeper, gamekeeper or maybe two, the lodge keeper, a shepherd, a gardener, and a cleaning company from Mircester comes in once a week. If he has a dinner party, he uses a catering firm. He owns the small village of Harby, more of a hamlet, and recently jacked up the rents, causing no end of ill will."

"How did you find out all this?"

"I phoned around," said Charles. "Let it go, Agatha. The suspects are legion."

Chapter Two

During the following week, Agatha found that she was too busy to even think about the death of Bellington. But on the Friday, she received a visit from Bellington's son, Damian.

He had a weak, almost feminine face and carefully waved fair hair. He was dressed in a light blue silk suit with three-quarter length sleeves over a white silk shirt open at the neck to display a gold medallion. His deep masculine voice came as a surprise.

"The police don't seem to be doing anything, and I want to know who murdered my father," he said.

"I'm sorry for your loss," said Agatha.

"Don't be. I hated the old bastard. That's the point. Everyone's heard me complaining about the old sod and wishing he were dead. I feel if I'm called in for questioning one more time, I'll have the screaming ab-dabs. So I want you to find out who did it."

"I'll do my best," said Agatha. "My secretary, Mrs. Freedman, will get you to sign the necessary contracts. Now, do you suspect anyone yourself?"

"Too many people had it in for him. First, the villagers didn't like their rents being jacked up. Then there were the allotment people."

"It seems to me," said Agatha cautiously, "that it would need to be someone who was in the house and could doctor the drinks unobserved. What about your sister?"

"Andrea? No. She must be the only one in mourning. We had the funeral yesterday, and hers were the only wet eyes around."

"What about your mother?"

"Too pissed to care. Drunk as a skunk most of the time. And she never went near him after the divorce. That was ten years ago. Why he fought for custody of us is beyond me. But I suppose he adored Andrea."

"What about the staff? I would like to arrange a meeting with them."

"Come down tomorrow. Say, ten in the morning. I'll have them gathered together."

After he had left and Agatha's detectives had returned for the Friday-night briefing, Agatha told them about the agency's latest client. Toni Gilmour, young, blond and beautiful, said, "We've got so much work already. Have you thought of employing another detective?"

"I'll think about it," said Agatha. Perhaps Gerald might like some temporary employment and they would become close and he would propose marriage and . . .

Patrick Mulligan, former police officer, broke into her dreams. "I could get a retired detective."

"I'll let you know after the week-end," said Agatha.

Simon Black, young with a jester's face and black hair, said eagerly, "Would you like me to come with you tomorrow?"

"No, I'll go on my own," said Agatha.

Phil Marshall, her oldest detective who lived in Carsely, knew all about Gerald Devere and guessed at Agatha's plans. In the past, Agatha had always chased after any attractive man who arrived in Carsely or in any of the nearby villages.

Agatha rushed home to her cottage to put on a slinky black wool dress and high heels. She sprayed herself liberally with Miss Dior and headed for Gerald's cottage.

But before she reached it, she met Mrs. Bloxby, who was hurrying along the road, her head bent. "I was going to ask Mr. Devere something," said Mrs. Bloxby in a flat voice. "But he was in the garden and otherwise occupied."

"I'm just on my way to see him," said Agatha. "How otherwise occupied?"

"I was about to ring the front doorbell when I heard his voice coming from the back garden. I walked around. He was kissing that newcomer, Miss Peta Currie. I backed off and left."

"That's fast work," said Agatha bitterly. "I've seen this Peta Currie with Gerald, and I met her at the allotments."

"Arrived a few months ago. Has an allotment. Rumoured to have been married but calls herself 'miss.'"

And here we are, thought Agatha sadly. Two middle-aged women looking as if they had just been jilted. "Like to come back to my place for a drink?" she asked.

"No, thank you. I'd better get back to the vicarage."

Agatha had decided to take Toni with her. Damian greeted them at the hall and said the staff were all waiting for them in the library. "When you're finished," he said, "Mother would like to see you."

"She's here!" exclaimed Agatha.

"Yes, I got her back. The place is mine now," said

Damian. "I can't be bothered with running it, but Mother is a great organiser."

Agatha thought this did not tally with Damian's earlier description of his mother as a drunk and said so. "She's taken the cure," said Damian. "Good rehab job, and she's my mother. You'd better talk to the factor first, Giles Bennet. He had a row with Dad. Dad accused him of fiddling the books to line his own pockets. He was given a month's notice. I kept him on because I got the accountants to go through the books and there was no evidence of fiddling."

Agatha found the interviews with the factor and the staff a waste of time. People had either been warned or did not like to speak ill of the dead, and they all said, even the factor, that he had been a model employer. Giles Bennet said that there had been nothing new in Lord Bellington firing him. It had happened regularly and he paid no attention to it. His lordship had been a great character. As the eulogies went on, Toni caught a look of malicious glee on Damian's face, quickly supressed when he saw her looking at him.

They were then led to a morning room where Olivia, Lady Bellington, was waiting for them. Agatha thought that it was only the ex-wives of Scottish peers who were allowed to retain their titles but, with unusual tact, refrained from saying so. Olivia was a tall, thin haggard woman with brown hair and large grey eyes. She was dressed in a faded blouse and jeans.

"So grateful for your help, Miss Prune," she said languidly.

"It's Raisin. Agatha Raisin."

"Sorry. I knew it was one of those wrinkled fruits. Have a seat. I don't know if I can help you because, as you probably know, I haven't seen Arthur in yonks."

"And you definitely had not seen anything of your husband since the divorce?"

"Not a sausage, darling. I mean his behaviour was gothic. Absolutely shiters."

"If the antifreeze could have been inserted in one of the bottles," said Toni, "might there not be some in other bottles?"

"Oh, my dear girl," said Damian, "the forensic lot went through the cellar end to end. Dad likes sweet stuff. He had been drinking Sauternes and crème de menthe. But could they find those bottles? Disappeared. Not even in the rubbish."

"It must have been someone with access to the hall," said Agatha. "It can't have been any of the villagers, for example."

"It could," said Damian. "Two days before he died, there was open day at the hall. You know the sort of thing. Marquees on the lawn. Stands with homemade cakes and stuff. White elephant stall. Yawn. I wasn't there. Andrea told me about it."

"Your sister? Is it possible to talk to her?" asked Agatha.

"She's off hiking in Scotland. I'll let you know when she gets back."

"Is there any of the villagers who was really furious at the rents going up?" asked Toni.

"Nasty old codger called Humphrey Sanders. Lives in Pear Tree cottage next to the pond."

"Well, that was a waste of space," said Agatha bitterly as they drove down to the village.

"Not quite," said Toni. "Damian is somehow enjoying our failure at getting anywhere." She told Agatha about the look she had surprised on his face.

"You don't hire a detective of my calibre if you're a murderer," said Agatha.

"It's happened before," said Toni. "They did it to hide the fact they were guilty."

"That was ages ago," said Agatha huffily. "I wish I weren't so worried about Mrs. Bloxby."

"Why?"

"Shouldn't have mentioned it. Here's that cottage and here goes for another useless interview."

The vicar looked up from his newspaper as his wife walked into the sitting room and slumped down in an armchair. "You looked tired," he said.

"That's all I need," said his wife bitterly.

"You've been working too hard," said the vicar. "And you've been looking so attractive lately. Tell you what. Let's go out to that new restaurant in Ancombe."

The sun slowly began to dawn in the gloomy night of Mrs. Bloxby's mind.

"That would be lovely."

Humphrey Sanders opened the door of his cottage. "I ain't buying nothing."

"I am a private detective," said Agatha, handing him her card. "I am investigating the murder of Lord Bellington."

"And good riddance," he said, and slammed the door.

"I'm sick of this," said Agatha. "Let's find a pub."

The village did not boast a pub, but they found one in a nearby village and settled down in the garden to eat fish and chips.

"That's better," sighed Agatha, pushing her plate away. "What did you make of Damian?"

"Effeminate, malicious, hiding something," said Toni.

"Now, Bellington said to me and Charles something

about changing his will," said Agatha. "That would be a motive. I wish for the umpteenth time I had the powers of the police." She took out her mobile and called Patrick. "See if any of your police contacts can tell you if Bellington meant to change his will," she asked.

Agatha lit a cigarette. "I'd forgotten something. Bellington had a mistress, Jenny Coulter. I'll need her address."

"Want to go back to Harby and knock on a few doors?" asked Toni.

"Fed up with the place. This is Sunday, and I dragged you down here. Maybe you had a date or something."

"Not at the moment," said Toni.

Agatha studied her assistant's beautiful face. She herself had not had a normal youth. Mostly, she had been too driven by ambition to think about finding dates.

"Do you ever try these dating agencies online?" asked Agatha.

"Haven't so far," said Toni.

"I think we should head back to Mircester and try to see Bill Wong. With any luck this is his day off and he might give us some information. At least the murder isn't in the Cotswolds and the villagers of Carsely can't accuse me of being a harbinger of death."

There was one allotment going spare. It had belonged to an elderly man who had died six months before. Hot contestants for the plot were Bunty Daventry, Josephine Merriweather and Harry Perry. But the head of the Small Allotments' Committee, Tommy Bennet, had held out against them, saying the plot should go to someone new.

"Look at it!" raged Bunty. "Full of weeds and the seeds blowing all over the place. It's a disgrace. Wait a bit! Look at that! Someone's been digging."

She walked over to the allotment. "Looks like a grave," she said.

"Probably is," said Harry. "You'd never believe the number of people who want to bury a pet. It's been dug fresh, like." He seized his spade. "I'm going to dig it up and see if I recognise the creature, and if I do, I'll take the dead beast and chuck it in their garden."

He dug energetically, his old walnut face creased in concentration. "Something soft here." He got down on his hands and knees and began to scrape away the earth with his fingers. Other allotment holders began to crowd around.

He suddenly fell back on his bottom while Bunty let out a scream of terror. Exposed was the white, dead face of Peta Currie. A little breeze had sprung up, and granules of earth rolled down the dead face like tears. Bunty, who had always prided herself on being stronger than any man, fainted. Mobile phones were snatched out all round as babbling voices shrieked for the police and ambulance.

Unaware of the drama, Agatha and Toni were sitting in a pub in Mircester with Bill. He had been on duty, and they had caught him just as he was leaving headquarters.

"You know I cannot discuss police business with you, Agatha," he was saying.

"Surely you can tell us if Bellington meant to disinherit Damian before he died," said Agatha. She studied his face. Something flickered in Bill's almond shaped eyes.

"So he did!" exclaimed Agatha with one of her unnerving flashes of intuition.

"I didn't say that." Bill's mobile rang. "I'd better take this." He walked away from the table.

Agatha heard him exclaim. "Carsely! Are you sure?" And then, "I'll be right there."

"I've got to go," he said when he returned to their table.

"What's happened in Carsely?" demanded Agatha.

"Never mind. See you. Thanks for the drink."

Agatha's brain was in a turmoil as she followed Bill's car to Carsely. It could be nothing to do with her or he would have taken her with him. Was it something to do with Bellington's murder? Several police cars raced past her.

When she got to Carsely, Agatha said, "They're all heading for the allotments. What on earth is happening? If we hadn't just seen Damian, I would expect something nasty to have happened to him."

She pulled up behind the police cars. She and Toni got out and hurried forward to find their way blocked by a policeman at the entrance to the allotments. "Can't go in there," he said.

"But there are people in there," protested Agatha.

"They were at the scene. Got to be interviewed."

"What scene? What happened?" demanded Agatha.

"Clear off and mind your own business."

They moved a little away. Then Agatha saw Mrs. Bloxby hurrying along the road, accompanied by Gerald.

"Isn't it terrible?" she said, coming up to them. "Poor Miss Currie."

"What?" demanded Agatha. "Never say someone's bumped her off."

"It appears she had been struck on the back of the head, and then the body was buried in one of the allotments," said the vicar's wife.

"How did you find out?" asked Toni.

"Two of the allotments holders phoned the vicarage as soon as the body was found," said Mrs. Bloxby.

Agatha's bearlike eyes fastened on Gerald's face.

"The police will want to know who was the last person who saw her alive," she said.

"Naturally," said Gerald stiffly. "That is normal procedure. Excuse me. Got to go home. Forgotten something."

Mrs. Bloxby put a hand on Agatha's arm and looked steadily at her face. She doesn't want me to talk about him kissing Peta last night, thought Agatha. Damn! Why? Loyalty to her friend kept her silent as she watched Gerald walk quickly away.

"So another murder," said a familiar voice behind Agatha. She swung round to find Charles. "Who's been bumped off?"

"Peta Currie," said Agatha. "Remember, we met her? Found in a grave on the allotments."

Charles studied the allotment holders. "Now there's a cross-section of village society," he remarked. "There are the old guard. Some of them look as if they've come out of *Planet of the Apes*. You see those sort of faces in old Victorian photographs. Those big simian mouths. Right into the twentieth century, it was so unfashionable to have a large mouth that women cursed with one would paint little rosebud mouths in the middle of it. Some middle-class women who look like militant vegetarians. Some genuine gardeners. And look! Over there. There's even a vineyard belonging to two attractive ladies. Do you know who they are?"

"One's a terribly good photographer," said Phil Marshall, who had walked up to join them. "And her friend is a tennis coach."

"How fascinating they all are," said Charles. "What did Peta do, I wonder, to cause her death? Step on someone's prize leeks?"

"I checked up on her last night," said Mrs. Bloxby. "I couldn't sleep. I wondered if there was anything on Google. In her early twenties, she was a famous model. She's been married and divorced three times."

"One up on you, Aggie," said Charles. "You've only managed two husbands."

"Any connection to Lord Bellington?" asked Agatha.

"Her first marriage was to a cousin of Lord Bellington's, a member of Parliament, Mr. Nigel Farraday."

"We'd better tell Bill," said Agatha. She walked to the policeman at the gate. "Tell Detective Sergeant Wong that Agatha Raisin has important information concerning the murder," she said. He turned away and spoke rapidly into a gadget on his lapel.

Agatha waited impatiently. At last, Bill came hurrying up and listened while she told him what Mrs. Bloxby had found out. "It's a tenuous connection," he said. "Come with me, Mrs. Bloxby, and we'll take a statement. Stay where you are, Agatha, and I'll call on you later."

Pink in the face with embarrassment, Mrs. Bloxby

followed Bill into the allotments. I wonder how she's going to explain her interest in Peta, thought Agatha.

She turned to Charles. "Let's go home and wait for Bill. What about you and Phil, Toni?"

Toni said she would like to get back to Mircester, and Phil pointed to his camera with the zoom lens and said he would wait and get as many photos of the allotment holders as he could.

Agatha and Charles sat in the kitchen and waited for Bill. They had meant to sit in the garden, but the wind had become blustery and cold with dark little clouds scurrying over the sun. "Look at all the autumn leaves blowing all over the place," said Agatha. "Such a shame. It all seems to pass so quickly. I feel like getting a can of lacquer and sticking them on."

Agatha put her laptop on the kitchen table and switched it on. "Looking up Peta?" asked Charles.

"No, I'm looking up Bellington's mistress, Jenny Coulter. Let's see. Damn. Nothing at all. I'd better get her address from Damian. Are they still called mistresses these days?"

Charles shrugged. "Partners or significant others. There was an amusing letter in the *Times* from a man who said that in Australia, partners were referred to as 'de facto.' It was only after a while that he realised he wasn't being introduced to deaf actors."

Agatha phoned Damian and asked for Jenny Coulter's whereabouts and then scribbled down an address. Then she told him about the death of Peta Currie.

"Who's she?" asked Damian.

"She was married to your father's cousin, Nigel Farraday, at one time."

"I think I met Nigel once when I was a child," said Damian. "Can't remember this Peta. I'll check up for you. But allotments are war zones. Got some in the village. Someone left the tap running last year, so the committee decided everyone had to carry water from a standpipe instead of plugging in their hoses. All because just one person was careless. Caused no end of fights."

The doorbell rang and Charles went to answer it. Agatha heard Bill's voice, told Damian she would talk to him later, and rang off.

Bill came into the kitchen followed by the pretty detective, Alice Peterson. He questioned Agatha closely about her visit to Harby Hall, and then said, "What's this I hear about Mrs. Bloxby?"

"What on earth is there to hear?" demanded Agatha defensively.

"The gossip at the allotments is that Mrs. Bloxby was smitten by Gerald Devere and that Gerald Devere had become romantically involved with Peta Currie."

"Rubbish!"

"That Mrs. Bloxby was seen spending a lot of time in his company, that she had taken to wearing smart new clothes, dying her hair and wearing make-up."

"Oh, that's my fault," lied Agatha. "I had been encouraging her for ages to do something about her appearance, and she at last took my advice. Mrs. Bloxby spends a lot of time with newcomers to the village to help them get settled in. Come on, Bill! Mrs. Bloxby is a saint."

"Nonetheless, when I have finished here, I will be talking to her. Where's Charles?"

Agatha looked around. "He was here a moment ago. Do you think there is some connection between Peta's murder and that of Lord Bellington?"

"Early days," said Bill.

Charles had slipped out to rush up to the vicarage. Fortunately, the vicar was out. Mrs. Bloxby listened in dismay as Charles warned her that Bill would be calling on her soon and the reason for his visit.

"What am I to say?" asked the distressed vicar's wife.

"You will tell him what Agatha told him moments ago, that she had been encouraging you to smarten yourself up and you finally took her advice. Gerald called on you a lot because he didn't know anyone in the village and you were helping him to get established. Okay?"

"But that would be a lie."

"Do you want to upset your husband? What if he returns when Bill is here? I'm afraid the village is buzzing with gossip about you and Gerald."

"I have been very silly," said Mrs. Bloxby in a low voice. "Mr. Devere paid me many compliments. It was so nice to be admired. I thought my husband never really noticed me. But he did, finally. Last night! He took me out for dinner and said I was doing too much and told me to hire a cleaner."

"Do you know how long Gerald had been romancing Peta?"

She shook her head. "I didn't know a thing about it until I caught them kissing. Did Ms. Raisin tell you about that?"

"Not yet. You know, I think men like Devere go around romancing women to boost their own ego. I hope someone kills him!"

The doorbell rang. "That'll be Bill," said Charles. "I'll go out through the churchyard."

Chapter Three

When Charles joined Agatha back in her kitchen, she said, "Damian called back with Jenny Coulter's address. She's in Mircester. Great! Let's see if she's at home."

"It's been a long day, Agatha," said Charles. "Can't you leave it until morning?"

"She's probably got a job. These days, so-called 'kept women' usually work as well."

"Speaking from experience?"

"I wish. You know, Charles, those allotments do have a certain charm."

"Like dead bodies?"

"No, I mean, I can see myself sitting outside a shed on a summer's day, watching things grow."

"The only thing you're likely to grow is boredom," said Charles. "You know, Aggie, you wrap yourself in fantasy so many times, I find it hard to believe that you can actually wake up to the real world and solve cases."

"I don't fantasise!" shouted Agatha. "And don't call me Aggie! Okay, Monday. Will you call at the office?"

"No, I will not. I do have a life of my own. I have to supervise arrangements for the harvest festival. Nice and bucolic and dead-body free."

When he had left, Agatha went to let her cats in. They eyed her sulkily because it had begun to rain. The fine weather had broken at last. Agatha looked at the clock. Ten in the evening! And she hadn't eaten. She lifted the lid of the freezer chest and stared bleakly at a pile of microwave dinners before slamming it shut again.

The doorbell rang. Agatha looked down at her cats. If Bill or Charles had come back, with that odd sense of theirs, they would have run to the door, but both continued to groom themselves.

She looked through the spy hole and saw Gerald on her doorstep. She reluctantly opened the door to one shattered dream.

"Is this too late?" asked Gerald.

"No. Come in. What's the matter?" said Agatha, leading the way to the kitchen. She felt no urge to excuse herself and go upstairs to refresh her make-up. That dream had died.

"Coffee? Or something stronger?" she offered.

"Nothing for me."

"So what's the problem? I assume you do have a problem."

Gerald sighed and sat down at the kitchen table. Agatha sat opposite him.

"Being in the force in an odd sort of way cushions one from the outside world. Us and them. Now I am one of them. My vanity has taken a strong blow. Peta came on to me with all guns blazing, and I was comforted and flattered. She has been murdered, and I seem to be prime suspect."

"Wilkes makes everyone feel like prime suspect," said Agatha bitterly. "You want something from me. What is it?"

"I want to work again. I was hoping you might need another detective."

Agatha was about to refuse. She was still cross with him for having upset Mrs. Bloxby. Then common sense came to her aid. Here was a man, suspect or not, who would have better contacts in the police than Patrick.

"Call at the office tomorrow at nine o'clock," she said, "and sign the necessary papers. I am going to see

Jenny Coulter, Bellington's ex-mistress, tomorrow. You can start by coming with me."

"Thank you."

"There is just one thing." Agatha's bearlike eyes bored into his face. "No more chatting up Mrs. Bloxby and giving her wrong ideas."

"I promise you I won't go near the vicarage again."

"Oh, yes, you jolly well will, but when her husband is there. It would be hurtful to cut her off. Invite Mrs. Bloxby and her husband to dinner."

"I'll do that. What must you think of me?"

Agatha grinned. "Not much as a man, but as a detective, I'd like to see how you do."

When he had left, that old romantic fantasy about him hovered over Agatha's head. She shook it violently as if to shake the nonsense away and went up to bed. But before she drifted off to sleep, she hoped that when Charles found out that Gerald had joined her staff, he would be annoyed.

Gerald was introduced to Agatha's staff the next morning. Agatha noticed as he shook hands all round that he held on to Toni's hand a little longer than was necessary.

Then they had a quarrel in the car park outside. Gerald insisted they should take his car, but Agatha wanted to start off being the one in control and won the battle. She drove off with a rather sulky Gerald beside her in the passenger seat.

"This place where she lives," said Agatha, "is in one of the council estates on the edge of town. I would have expected her to live somewhere better."

"Maybe she relied on Bellington for money and a home, I wonder what she looks like," said Gerald, after Agatha had parked the car and they were walking towards the entrance to the flats. "I got photos of Bellington at various functions e-mailed to me from an old contact. His ex is in a lot of the old ones, but in the newer ones, there's no sign of any love life."

Agatha felt a stab of envy. Of course he would have more useful contacts than she did herself. She often fretted at being kept out of police investigations, being left with no forensic details.

Jenny Coulter's flat was in a small block, only four stories high. Jenny's flat was on the top floor. There was an OUT OF ORDER sign on the lift. When they reached the top floor, Agatha found she was out of breath and that her feet hurt. Oh, God, she thought, here it comes at last. No more cigarettes and no more high heels. I'm doomed.

"Is anything the matter?" asked Gerald.

"What? No, I'm fine. Ring the bell."

Gerald pressed the bell. Then there was silence:

only the moaning sound of the wind which had risen outside. There were no usual sounds one would expect in a block of flats: no television sounds, crying babies or rowing couples. There were only two apartments to each floor. "I'll try the apartment opposite," said Agatha. At first, there seemed to be no one home there either, but just as Agatha was turning away, the door was opened by a very old man, leaning on two sticks. "Who is it, Grandpa?" called a voice behind him.

"I think it's the Jehovahs," he said. "Look here, I don't believe in God, never have, never will and . . ."

"We are private investigators," shouted Agatha. "Do you know when your neighbour, Miss Coulter, will be home?"

His pale, watery eyes stared at her. "I ain't deaf. She's usually home, but she don't answer the door if she thinks it's someone she don't know."

"Thank you," said Agatha, still cross at having been mistaken for a Jehovah's Witness.

Agatha took out a business card and shoved it through the letterbox. She rang the bell again. After a few minutes, when she was just about to give up, the door opened, and a plump woman with grey hair answered it. "I was hoping to speak to Miss Coulter," said Agatha.

"That's me. Is it about that mean old bastard?"

"Yes, if you mean Lord Bellington."

"Come in."

They followed her into her living room. Agatha introduced Gerald. The room contained some nice pieces of antique furniture and a basketweave Sheraton sofa and chairs.

Jenny saw Agatha surveying the furniture and grinned. "When I left the old bastard, I got the removal lorry round first during the night. Left a note saying if he wanted his stuff back, he could sue me."

Gerald said, "Have you any idea who might have poisoned him?"

"I bet it was that son of his. Weird. The whole family's weird. Was the poison in one of his filthy-sweet drinks?"

"Yes," said Gerald. "It was either in the sweet wine or the crème de menthe. So it must have been someone who knew he liked sweet alcohol."

"He had a fete or some type of thing like that," said Agatha. "One of the villagers could have got into the house. I'm sure they used a lavatory in the house."

"He knew his drinking habits weren't fashionable," said Jenny. "Only the immediate family would know about his liking for sweet drinks."

"What about dinner parties?" asked Gerald.

"Only the best wine and port afterwards," said Jenny. "I told all this to the police. They tracked me down pretty quickly. I have an alibi for the night he was murdered, but it was pointed out to me that a bottle of wine or crème de menthe could have been poisoned any time before."

"This is a council flat," said Agatha. "Was it hard to find?"

"I've always had it. Hung on to it for a rainy day. Never thought the storm would arrive, but here I am. Have a seat."

Agatha was puzzled. She had expected someone like the few trophy wives who lived in Carsely: blond, cosmetically enhanced and each with her personal trainer. Jenny certainly had a figure to delight an Edwardian gentleman, having a generous bosom and large hips. Her eyes were large and brown. But she had deep grooves at the side of her mouth and wrinkles radiating above her lips and around her eyes. She came to the conclusion that Jenny had once been a looker in her younger days, and that would be when the affair started.

"How did you meet Lord Bellington?" she asked.

"Let me see. That would be about five years ago. I was working in a jewellers in the town, and he came in to buy a pendant for his daughter. We got talking, and he took me for dinner. The affair took off from there. At first he was very generous, and it was fun living in a big house. I was between men. The one before him had turned mean and bullying. Then, guess what? Bellington turned mean and bullying. Men!"

"Have you always been an . . . er . . . mistress?" asked Gerald.

"I suppose so. I've had the benefits of marriage but the freedom to clear off when I felt like it."

Agatha surveyed her curiously. What on earth did she *do* that made her so evidently popular? It was all a puzzle.

"Did you ever meet Nigel Farraday?" she asked.

"A few times."

"You see," said Agatha. "Peta Currie was murdered in the village of Carsely. She was married to him at one time."

"I read about that," said Jenny. "I never met the girl. Before my time and I didn't like Nigel. He treated me like dirt, and his wife is a pill."

"I looked up their address," said Gerald. "They live in Iddington Loxby. Is that near Harby?"

"It's about six miles away," said Jenny. "I haven't offered you anything. Would you like coffee or something?"

"No, we'd better be on our way," said Agatha. "He's a member of Parliament, isn't he?"

"Yes, he stands as an Independent. He was a Conservative and he feared he might lose his seat, so he decided to leave the party and stand as an Independent, promising all things to all people with nostalgia thrown in. You know, Britain for the British, throw all the immigrants out, bring back smoking, and double the pension money for the elderly. And as he is never likely to have any real power, he can promise what he likes."

As they were driving off, Agatha said, "I expected someone more glamorous."

"Oh, she's sexy," said Gerald.

"I wouldn't know," commented Agatha huffily. What an odd world it was! Women's magazines told you to wear heels and perfume, hair extensions and false eyelashes to lure the male creature, and here you have a woman like someone's mother. She wondered if she would ever experience sex combined with tenderness and romance. James Lacey belonged to the wham-bang school. Charles was an expert lover, but always self-contained. "Like being shagged by the cat."

"What?" demanded Gerald, and Agatha realised to her horror that she had spoken aloud.

"Nothing," said Agatha quickly. "Thinking about an old case."

They finally reached the village of Iddington Loxby. Gerald stopped by the village green and asked a man where they could find the home of Mr. Farraday.

"That's Coddend Manor," he said. "Go back the

way you came and turn left at the sign that says Cod-dend. You'll see the gates a little bit along that road. Got pineapples on the gateposts."

Soon they were cruising up a long narrow drive, thickly wooded on either side. The car bumped over a cattle grid, and they were out of the shelter of the trees and found open fields on either side. Agatha drove round a stable block, through an arch and into a court-yard which was full of cars.

"He must have guests," said Gerald. "Look! There's a space over there. Back into it."

"This car goes forwards. It doesn't go back," said Agatha, who hated reversing. She parked between a Rolls and a Bentley.

"Looks as if it was once a nice Georgian house. Now it's got odd Victorian bits tagged on. And look at all that ivy! Must be eating into the stonework."

The door was standing open. Agatha was about to walk straight in, but Gerald caught her arm. "Shouldn't we ring and get the butler to announce us?"

"I think hardly anyone but the very rich have but-lers these days. Come on."

They found themselves in a passage leading to a T-junction with corridors going off to left and right.

"Maybe we should have phoned," said Gerald.

"As an ex-copper you should know it's often better to surprise them," retorted Agatha.

Gerald stopped short. His face was creased up with anger. "I know more about detecting than you could ever learn!" he shouted.

"Oh, shut up, you pompous git!" yelled Agatha.

A woman appeared at the end of the corridor. She looked so like Peta that Agatha's heart gave a lurch. "Who the hell are you?" she demanded, "and what are you doing in my house?"

Agatha hurried forward with a placatory smile. "I am Private Detective Agatha Raisin. I am investigating the murder of Peta Currie. It would be helpful to learn something about her background. We wondered if we could have a word with Mr. Farraday."

"It is not convenient. We have guests."

"What's up, darling?" A man walked towards them.

"This woman," said his wife in glacial tones, "wants to interview you about Peta Currie. I told her to get lost."

He walked forwards. He was a tall man with a thick head of white hair. His white face was marred with red splotches, and his large nose had very open pores.

"Don't worry, poppet," he said. "You look after our guests." He opened a door to the left. "In here."

The room had a dusty unused look. "Please sit down," he said.

Agatha sat on a battered sofa which sent up a puff of dust. Gerald sat beside her. Nigel pulled up a hardback chair, swung it round, sat down and leaned on the back. He was wearing a collarless shirt and baggy shorts. "My barbecue outfit," he said. "Now, you are?"

After introducing them both, Agatha began to question him about Peta. "There was nothing to her apart from clothes, make-up and a devouring interest in money. But she was attractive-looking, I'll grant you that," he said. "But she refused to breed. As a politician, it helps to have a family. The next one was a loser as well. Hit lucky with this one. Two little boys. What about you pair? Any kids?"

To Gerald's horror, Agatha said sorrowfully. "Gerald didn't want me to have any."

"Poor you. Now you're too old. You could adopt."

"Wait a moment!" howled Gerald. "I would have you know that I am a retired Scotland Yard detective, working for the Agatha Raisin Agency. We are not married. Agatha, what the hell came over you?"

Nigel leered at Agatha. "She's a kittenish joker. I like that."

Agatha smiled at him, and he stroked back his hair and smiled back. "So tell me a bit more. Was she faithful to you?"

"Not towards the end of our marriage. Lucky for me. Put a private detective on her and got enough evidence so that I didn't have to pay out oodles of cash when I divorced her."

"But was she someone who might be what we call a murderee? You know, did she frequent bad company? Drugs? Jealous lovers? Anything like that?"

"I was too busy with an election by the time she started being unfaithful. Tell you what, Agatha—I may call you Agatha?"

"Please do."

"Why don't we get together for dinner one evening? By that time, I'll have raked my poor brains for any stuff that might be useful to you."

"Fine," said Agatha.

Before they got into her car, Agatha slipped on the flat shoes she used for driving and tossed her high heels in the back.

"You know he only wants to get into your knickers," said Gerald.

"It happens from time to time," said Agatha. "But by the time he finds he's on a loser, I might get something useful out of him."

Gerald, in the passenger seat, looked sideways at Agatha as if seeing her for the first time. He eyed her long legs displayed under short skirt, her glossy hair, and was aware of the faint smell of French perfume which surrounded her.

"I didn't kiss Peta," he said. "She kissed me. She sat on my lap and kissed me before I knew what she meant to do."

"And did you cast her off, saying, 'I am not that kind of man?'"

"I didn't. I didn't see it coming. What man would?"

"I've got one friend who would see it coming a mile off," said Agatha, thinking of Charles. Where *was* Charles? She realised she would rather have Charles with her than Gerald and then gave herself a mental slap on the wrist. Charles came and went in her life, often as cool and detached as a cat.

"We'll see if Damian is at home," said Agatha. "Surely he must have heard some gossip about Peta. And I'd really like to interview the daughter."

To her surprise, when she parked the car, Gerald ran round to open the door for her.

They rang the bell and waited. The door was eventually opened by Lady Bellington. She greeted Agatha with, "Oh, you tiresome woman. First the police, now you. Still, if Damian wants you, I'll need to put up with it." She walked away from them, leaving the door open.

"Where is Damian?" called Agatha to her retreating back.

"Garden," Lady Bellington shouted over her shoulder before disappearing into a door and slamming it behind her.

Said Agatha to Gerald, "Instead of searching through this rabbit warren of a place to find a door leading to the garden, let's go out and walk round the building."

When they emerged, fitful sunlight was flickering through the ivy leaves covering the building. A chill breeze had sprung up. Agatha wished she had worn a coat. Then she realised she was still wearing the flat shoes she used for driving. She felt diminished and not only in height. But the gravel path around the house leading to the back would have been difficult to negotiate in high heels, so she walked on, trying not to feel dumpy.

They found Damian seated in a lounge chair on a terrace at the back of the house. A gust of wind sent a flurry of red and gold autumn leaves swirling about him. He caught one and held it up. "One of the lost children of the dying year," he said.

And what do you reply to that? Agatha wondered.

"Come and sit down," he said.

Agatha chose an upright metal garden chair, and Gerald perched on the edge of a lounger on the other side of Damian.

"So who's the murderer?" he asked.

"Early days," said Agatha. "Where is your sister, Andrea?"

"Got back yesterday. The funeral is tomorrow. What's left of dear old Dad, that is, after they've cut him up and extracted his bodily fluids."

"You weren't very fond of your father, were you?" asked Gerald.

"He could be tiresome. I had a poem published in The Spectator when I was only sixteen. I was so proud. I showed it to him. He punched me in the face and called me a poofter. He said if he caught me writing poetry, he would cut off my allowance. So that was the end of that."

"If you disliked him so much," said Agatha, "why are you so keen to find out who murdered him?"

He giggled. "Oh, you *are* a one, duckie. To shake the man by the hand. Seriously. I'm prime suspect, and I want you to get the police off my back."

"Does Andrea inherit anything?" asked Gerald.

"Her allowance, which is madly generous, has to go on being paid. But I wish she'd stop mooning about here and go somewhere, and stop moping around the place."

"We would like to speak to her," said Agatha.

"Whatever floats your boat, sweetie." He leaned back and shouted, "Mrs. Dinky!"

The name conjured up visions of a pretty little maid, but it was a small, aggressive-looking woman who appeared through the French windows. "Fetch Andrea, would you?" ordered Damian.

"Is that your housekeeper?" asked Agatha.

"Yes."

"But it's not the one I first interviewed."

"Sacked her. Malicious gossip. Dinky's from the village and knows how to keep her mouth shut, particularly as I own her cottage."

"Doesn't the sacked housekeeper live in your village?"

"Mrs. Bull? Yes, Ivy Cottage. Ah, here is my beloved sister. I'll leave you to it."

"Oh, so it's you." Andrea glared at Agatha and Gerald. "I was told a *lady* and a *gentleman* were waiting to see me. Mistake."

Despite the fact that her poor background had recently been spread about the village of Carsely, Agatha still had the fear that people might see through the façade she had built up of good clothes and posh accent to her origins in a Birmingham slum. She forced down a burst of bad temper and said, "We are trying to find out who murdered your father, and we would appreciate it if you could tell us if you can think of anyone who might have wanted to kill him."

Andrea started to walk away. "I know who killed him," she said over her shoulder.

"Wait!" cried Agatha. "Who is it?"

"Damian, of course."

Chapter Four

"Wait!" called Agatha, but Andrea ran off into the house.

Damian appeared through the French windows, and from the mocking smile on his face, Agatha guessed he had heard every word.

"So did you really kill your father?" asked Agatha.

"No, but Andrea would like to think so. The pair of you look quite shocked. Don't listen to her, or you'll never find who really bumped my father off."

"Why would Andrea want you to be the murderer?"

"Because all the inheritance would then go to her, wicked me not being able to profit from crime."

"I would like to talk to the housekeeper you sacked," said Agatha.

"Hoping that a disgruntled ex-employee will dish the dirt? As I told you, her name is Mrs. Bull, and she lives in Ivy cottage. It's right on the green. You can't miss it."

"Is there any chance of speaking to your sister again?" asked Gerald.

"Not a hope in hell. Run along and detect elsewhere."

Mrs. Bull looked like a gargoyle. Her ears stuck out a right angles, and she had a large nose and a curved-up mouth. Her eyes were green, the colour of sea-washed glass and just as opaque. She was very tall and thin. Agatha made the introductions.

"You'd best come in," she said. "I can tell you a thing or two about that lot."

She led the way into a dark parlour. Ivy Cottage lived up to its name. Ivy blocked most of the light from the windows. The room was cluttered with china ornaments, framed photographs, magazines and bunches of dried flowers. Mrs. Bull waved her hand to a horsehair sofa, indicating they should sit down. She switched on a fake log fire in the grate and then sat primly on the edge of a heavy Jacobean-type chair.

"Why were you sacked?" asked Agatha.

"I spoke to one of them reporters, and Mr. Damian sacked me."

"Aren't you frightened that he might take this cottage away from you if you talk to us?" asked Gerald.

"Can't. It's mine. The old man gave it to me. 'For services rendered,' he said." She let out a cackle of laughter. "First time I heard a bit o' leg over called that."

"You mean . . ." began Agatha.

"Screwed me rotten when he was drunk."

"Didn't Mr. Bull have something to say about that?"

"Ain't no Mr. Bull. I calls myself Mrs."

"But he had a mistress. What did Jenny have to say about that?"

"Wily bird that one. Didn't care. Said it gave her a night off."

"So have you any idea who murdered Lord Bellington?" asked Gerald.

"'Twas that ex-wife o' his. I'll tell you why. I caught her down in the cellars one evening with a syringe in her hand."

Agatha said, "But she is a recovering alcoholic and was probably into drugs. Maybe she was just down there to get a fix. But wait a minute. I gather she didn't come back to the hall until after Bellington died and Damian invited her."

"That's what I mean," said Mrs. Bull triumphantly. "Her had no cause to be there."

"And what did Lord Bellington say when you told him?"

"Didn't."

Agatha's bearlike eyes bored into her. "She paid you to keep quiet."

"Well, I didn't think her was up to anything nasty-like, and the money came in handy."

"So when was this?" asked Agatha.

"A week before he popped his clogs."

"Did you tell the police?"

"I thought I'd get into trouble."

"So why are you telling us?" asked Gerald.

"Someone called on the phone just afore you got here and said I'd better keep my mouth shut."

"A man or a woman?" asked Agatha.

"Couldn't say. Metallic sort of voice."

"But why didn't you tell the police about Lady Bellington and the syringe?" asked Gerald.

"Told you, didn't I? Don't have nothing to do with the police."

A phone rang shrilly from the back premises. "Better answer that," said Mrs. Bull. "Back in a mo."

"We'll have to tell the police," whispered Gerald.

"I think she's a fantasist. Why should Bellington

want to bed someone who looks like an extra in a horror movie?"

"He was drunk and she was available," said Gerald. "Shhh, she's coming back."

"You'd better leave," said Mrs. Bull. "Right now!"

"Who was on the phone?" asked Agatha.

"Friend in the village. Now, get out o' here."

"Agatha," said Gerald when they were clear of the village, "we really have to tell the police about her. They can check her phone. She was threatened. That last phone call really frightened her."

"I'll see if Bill Wong is at home," said Agatha reluctantly. "The last person I want to see is Wilkes. I think that wretched man likes dragging me in for questioning."

They managed to prise the information out of Mrs. Wong that her son was on duty until four o'clock in the afternoon. "We'll wait in the car park outside police headquarters and catch him when he leaves," said Agatha.

"I don't see why we are bothering with a mere detective sergeant," said Gerald.

"Because he's clever and he'll listen properly."

Bill came out of headquarters accompanied by Alice Peterson. They were laughing and chatting until Bill saw Agatha approaching and his face fell.

"I've discovered something important," said Agatha. "You've got to listen."

"All right," said Bill reluctantly. "Out with it." Gerald came to join them.

Bill listened intently as Agatha told him about what Mrs. Bull had said. When she had finished, Bill said, "You'll need to come in with me and make a statement, and then we'll get onto it right away."

"Do I have to see Wilkes?" asked Agatha.

"No, it's his day off. I'll take your statements, and then we'll go and see her."

After they had given their statements and were heading back to Carsely, Agatha said sulkily, "It looks as if we might have solved that murder and the police will take all the credit and Damian will be furious if the killer turns out to be his own mother."

"We've still got Peta's murder to solve," Gerald pointed out.

"And no one is paying us for that." She drove down into the village and turned into Lilac Lane. "There's smoke coming from James's chimney. He must be home."

"And there's Toni waiting on your doorstep," said Gerald, smoothing back his hair.

"Probably wants some girl talk, so you'd better be off," said Agatha. She was aware that Toni had, in the past, betrayed a liking for much older men. She parked outside her cottage. Gerald nipped out and said something to Toni, who shook her blond head.

"What was that about?" asked Agatha, after Gerald had left.

"Wanted to take me out for dinner," said Toni.

"Old lecher," grumbled Agatha. "What brings you?"

"A quiet Sunday so I thought I'd take a run over to Carsely and see how you are getting on."

"Come in and I'll tell you all about it."

Agatha had just finished talking when the doorbell rang. It was Simon Black. "Thought I'd drop in," he said.

"Meaning you are in pursuit of Toni. Give up, Simon."

"Well, if that's your attitude. . . . Actually, I'm not. Boring old day."

"Oh, come in. She's in the kitchen." The doorbell rang again. "Now, who is it?" demanded Agatha.

This time it was her former employee, Roy Silver, and behind him stood James Lacey. "This is getting to be a party," said Agatha.

When they were all seated in the kitchen, she told her adventures over again. "Have the press been round?" asked Roy eagerly.

"No, Roy, so you've had a wasted visit. Is that the reason you came?"

"I need your help," said Roy. His pasty face had

a new crop of pimples which always happened when he was upset. "Pedman is threatening to sack me." Pedman was Roy's public-relations boss.

"Why?"

"I punched a reporter on the nose."

"Which one?"

"Bert Cunningham."

The top reporter on the *Sketch*? How come?"

"I've been handling that pop group, Drop Dead Gorgeous. The lead singer, Jez Honor, has been charged with raping a fourteen-year-old."

"Pedman should have stopped representing them."

"Well, they didn't, and I got stuck with the damage limitation. I was keeping the press at bay and Cunningham called me a fairy so I punched him on the nose."

"But you are a . . ." Agatha bit her lip. "Have you got what he said on tape?"

"Yes, I taped what was supposed to be a press conference. He's suing me, Aggie, and Pedman is furious."

"Oh, talk among yourselves, you lot, while I deal with this," said Agatha.

She returned to the kitchen after half an hour, saying wearily, "Well, that's fixed. You aren't being sued, and you're to go to work tomorrow as usual."

Roy began to sob with relief. He said when he could, "How did you manage it?"

"I got Cunningham at home and said if he didn't drop it, I would have him damned as a homophobe. I phoned Pedman and told him Cunningham was dropping the action and he should tell that pop group that as it was all at the moment sub judice, Pedman could not represent them until after the court case. You are to take over Comfy Baby nappies."

"Oh, God! Mary Dobbs was doing that. Why am I landed arranging photo shoots with squalling brats and mothers from hell?"

"Because she handed in her notice, that's why. Be grateful."

"I am. Honest. Thanks, Agatha."

"Where's James?"

"Gone home," said Toni.

Agatha slumped down onto a chair at the kitchen table. "Simon. Fix me a gin and tonic and get something for yourself and Toni."

Toni watched Agatha taking out a packet of cigarettes. "Still smoking," she commented.

"So bloody what?" demanded Agatha harshly. "This is my first cigarette today."

She lit up, inhaled and immediately felt dizzy. Agatha made a promise to herself that she would never go without fags for a long time because the first one always had a bad effect.

After all, she had tried to give up so many times, and what a waste of space that had turned out to be.

The doorbell shrilled, making her jump. "That'll probably be James," she said.

She patted her hair in the hall mirror. Even though one had lost interest in one's ex, it doesn't do to give them the pleasure of looking frazzled. But her heart sank as she opened the door to be confronted by not only Bill, but Inspector Wilkes as well.

"This is a serious business," said Wilkes ponderously.

"Oh, stop glooming at me on the doorstep and come in," said Agatha.

"Mr. Devere will be joining us," said Wilkes.

In the kitchen, Agatha said, "Toni, this is going to take some time. Why don't you and Simon go to the pub?"

After they had left, Wilkes produced Agatha and Gerald's statements. At that moment, Gerald walked into the kitchen. "Toni let me in," he said. "What's happening?"

"Just about to find out," said Agatha.

"Mrs. Bull has disappeared," said Wilkes.

"Are you sure?" said Gerald. "She may have gone to a friend's house."

"Her door was unlocked. All her things are there

including her handbag. We interviewed Lady Bellington. She insists the woman was talking rubbish. The week before Lord Bellington's murder, she was in a rehab in Oxford. No record of her leaving the building. Plenty of witnesses to swear she was there the whole time."

"Mrs. Bull got a phone call when we were there," said Agatha. "When she came back, she looked frightened. You will see from our reports that she had already been threatened."

"We're checking her phone line," said Bill.

Roy interrupted them. "I've got to go. Bye, Aggie."

"Don't call me . . . Oh, what's the use?" Agatha turned to Wilkes. "I can't think of anything else other than what I said in my statement."

"Right," said Wilkes. "A word with you in private, Mr. Devere."

When Gerald had left with Wilkes, Agatha said, "What's he up to, Bill?"

"He was grumbling about a detective like Devere working with you. Perhaps he is frightened you will solve the murders."

They then sat in silence until Wilkes eventually returned with Gerald and said they were leaving. After they had gone, Agatha asked, "Well, Gerald, what was that all about?"

"He said he had had a word with the superintendent, and the police would like to employ me on this case in an advisory capacity. So I won't be working for you."

"You signed a contract," said Agatha. "I've a good mind to keep you to it. No, on second thoughts, just get lost!"

Toni and Simon, instead of going to the pub, had made their way to the allotments to see if they could find out anything. When they arrived, allotment holders were gathered on the road outside. A full moon lit up the angry faces. Harry Perry was shouting that one of them had stolen his prize marrow. "I blame you, Bunty Daventry," he was yelling. "You was always jealous of my fame."

"It's only a poxy marrow," sneered Josephine Merriweather.

"If you were a man," raged Harry, "I'd beat the living daylights out of you."

"Oh, you would, would you?" Josephine advanced on him, waving her fists.

"Calm down all of you," said one of the older members, Fred Palmer. "Fighting ain't getting us anywhere. Have you called the police, Harry?"

" 'Course I did, and they won't do anything. I wanted a house-to-house search."

"Aren't we forgetting about Peta's murder?" asked Bunty.

"I'm not forgetting," said Harry. "But she wasn't much use as a gardener anyway. The theft of my marrow is more important."

Toni and Simon walked away from the angry voices. "Allotments seem to bring out the worst in people," said Simon. "You'd think they'd all be rejoicing now that their precious plots aren't to be destroyed. Why don't we go to the pub?"

Toni hesitated. "Maybe I should go back to Agatha."

"It's all right. I'm in love," said Simon.

Toni smiled with relief. She had become weary of Simon's pursuit of her. "All right. The pub it is. Who's the lucky lady?"

"Alice Peterson."

"*Detective* Alice Peterson? Oh, Simon. Bill's keen on her but can't do anything because of them being colleagues. He'll be furious. How long have you been dating her?"

"Well, I haven't asked her out yet. I'm waiting for the right moment."

"Don't do it. You'll only hurt Bill."

"He can't do anything about asking her out and I can," said Simon mulishly. "I know where she lives. I'm going to wait outside her house and just ask her."

"Oh, forget about the pub," snapped Toni and strode off, autumn leaves swirling about her feet in a rising wind.

Later that evening, like a dog waiting for its master, Simon lurked outside the block of flats where Alice lived. At last he saw her driving up with Bill and moved into the shadows. His heart beat fast as he watched her leaning into the car to say goodnight.

Bill drove off. As Alice approached the entrance, Simon stepped forward.

"Good evening," he said.

Alice looked puzzled for a moment as she studied his face in the entrance light. Then her face cleared. "Oh, it's you, Simon. Found anything out?"

"Nothing much," said Simon. "I wondered if you would care to go for a drink?"

"It's eleven o'clock at night and I'm tired," said Alice, beginning to walk away.

"Another time?" called Simon. But Alice did not reply. The entrance door slammed behind her. I'd forgotten how late it was, mourned Simon. I'll send her flowers. That should do the trick.

Agatha was about to set out for Harby Hall the next morning to try to interview Andrea and find out if she had any proof to back up her allegation that her brother had murdered their father. She had not told Wilkes about Andrea's startling accusation. Maybe Gerald had told them. Agatha did not like the idea of the police knowing absolutely everything. Then she had to find out what had happened to Mrs. Bull.

Charles appeared as she was about to set out. She wanted to tell him huffily that she did not need his help, but stopped herself in time. She told him instead all she had learned.

They were just about to leave when Agatha's mobile rang. It was Bill Wong. "Is Simon Black there?" he asked.

"He's out looking for a lost teenager," said Agatha. "Why?"

"He's stalking Alice."

"What?"

"He was lurking outside her building late last night, and he's just sent her flowers."

"Is she complaining about him?"

"Well, no."

"I can't do anything about it, Bill, unless she's angry."

"Look, we're friends, Agatha. Tell him to stop!"

"Oh, all right. I'll try. Simon gets crushes on women, but it soon blows over."

"Why doesn't Bill ask her out himself?" asked Charles, after Agatha had told him about the phone call.

"Police regulations."

"I'm sure other coppers never bother about them."

"I'm sure, even if he did try to date her, that mother of his would soon find a way to put a stop to it."

Mrs. Wong was at that moment returning with a shopping bag over her arm. Her neighbour, Mrs. Golightly, hailed her. "Cold day," she called. "They say it's going to be a hard winter. Had the grandchildren down for the week-end. Little darlings. You got any?"

"My son is not married as you very well know."

"What a pity. Doesn't fancy the ladies maybe?"

"Tcha!" Mrs. Wong marched up the garden path. In the past, she had always felt superior to Mrs. Golightly, whose son had done time for car theft. Her face burned red at the idea that her malicious neighbour might put it about that her precious Bill was . . . well . . . the-other-way inclined. Bill would need to get married and as soon as possible.

What an odd morning, thought Alice. First there was the bouquet from Simon, and Mrs. Wong had phoned to ask her for supper. Alice was terrified of Bill's mother, and so she had lied and said she had a date. "So you're that kind of girl," Mrs. Wong had said. "Bill's better off without you."

Upset, Alice had phoned Bill on his mobile, knowing he had gone to Harby with Wilkes.

Bill adored his parents. He had hitherto been blind to his mother's habit of driving girlfriends away. Because of his Chinese father and his own slightly

Asian appearance, he had been bullied at school. Having a poor opinion of his looks, he assumed that, after a visit to his home, previous girlfriends had gone off him because of his lack of attraction. But now Bill, who had long adored Alice, was furious. He phoned his mother and said he was moving out to a flat of his own. If she had cried, he might have relented. But she cursed him for being an unnatural son, and so he cut her off in mid-rant and vowed to find a place to live as soon as he could. He then phoned Alice and apologised for his mother's behaviour and said he was moving out.

Alice, who had once had a miserable supper with the Wong family, was sympathetic. "There's a flat in my block available," she said. "I'll speak to the landlord today."

And Bill, who had been sent to the village of Harby to search for the missing Mrs. Bull, was elevated to a dream of living next door to Alice. Wasn't there a song about that, he wondered dreamily.

"Have you found her?" asked the familiar voice of Agatha Raisin behind him. He swung round to see Agatha and Charles.

"Not a sign of her," said Bill with a wide grin.

"So why are you looking so happy?"

"It's a lovely day to be out in the country."

Agatha looked up at the lowering black clouds and

then at the falling leaves driven by a brisk cold wind and said, "It's miserable. Never mind. Is Wilkes up at the hall?"

"Yes. He's interviewing Andrea."

"We should have beaten him to it, Charles," said Agatha. "I bet she denies the whole thing. So let's get back to Mrs. Bull. Say, she's been bumped off. Where would you dump a body, Bill?"

"Haven't a clue."

"What about the allotments?" asked Charles. "I saw them at the edge of the village."

"I'd better go on my own," said Bill. "If Wilkes turns up and finds you with me, he'll be furious. Oh, Lord, here come the press."

"You deal with them," said Agatha quickly. "Let's go, Charles."

Agatha and Charles drove to the allotments. Unlike the ones in Carsely, several of the plots were vacant and covered in weeds. There was no one in sight. They wandered through the allotments, looking to right and left. There were no signs of freshly turned earth: nothing that looked like a grave. The wind moaned through the trees bordering the allotments.

Agatha drew her fake fur coat tighter about her and shivered. "This place gives me the creeps. I seem to hear someone shouting, 'Help!'"

"There's an old well over in that far corner," said Charles.

"Looks as if it hasn't been used for a century," said Agatha. "I'm cold and hungry, and a gin and tonic is calling to me."

But Charles walked over to the well. It was covered with a stone slab. He leaned down and pressed his ear against it. Then he straightened up and called, "Get a tyre iron out of the car, Aggie! I swear I heard a moan. Bring a torch as well."

When Agatha came back, Charles inserted the tyre iron under the edge of the slab and heaved. The old slab split in two. He grasped the edge of one of the pieces and hauled it onto the grass. Then he took the torch from Agatha and shone it down into the well. The white face and terrified eyes of a woman stared up at him.

"I think we've found her," he said. "Phone Bill. Have a look. Is that Mrs. Bull?"

Agatha looked down at the terrified face. "It's her." She took out her mobile and called Bill. Then, leaning over the well, she shouted down, "Help is on its way. Who did this to you?"

But Mrs. Bull had relapsed into unconsciousness.

They were soon joined by Bill and several policemen and then by Wilkes. Before a fire engine arrived, Agatha fretted. If Mrs. Bull had been thrown into the well, she must be suffering from broken bones.

At last the firemen arrived. It was decided that the thinnest of the firemen should be lowered down with a canvas hoist to put around Mrs. Bull. An ambulance rolled up, and paramedics stood by.

At last, Mrs. Bull was slowly hoisted to the surface. She gave one long scream of agony and then fell silent.

Oh, let her stay alive, prayed Agatha as Mrs. Bull's white-and-blueish face appeared over the parapet of the well. Police had cordoned off the allotments, keeping the press at bay.

She was tenderly placed on a stretcher, an oxygen mask over her face and a drip in her arm.

Agatha scrolled down her phone until she found Damian's number. "I've got to speak to you. It's urgent."

"Come up to the house," he said. "What's happened?"

"Tell you when I get there," said Agatha. She rang off. "Come along, Charles."

"Not so fast," said Wilkes, looming over her. "I need statements from both of you as to why you so conveniently found the missing woman down the well."

"I have a job to do as well," said Agatha. "Charles and I will call in at headquarters and give you a full statement later on."

"You do that," said Wilkes, "and I will have you

arrested for impeding the police in their enquiries. Detective Wong! Take their statements . . . now!"

Bill was painstaking and meticulous. It took over an hour before they were finally able to leave and go to Harby Hall.

Chapter Five

Damian answered the door himself. "So Ma Bull has turned up her toes?" he said cheerfully.

"No, she is still alive," said Agatha. "How did you hear about it?"

"The jungle drums of Harby have been beating nonstop. Although I was told she was dead and buried in the allotment, just like Peta."

"Your jungle drums are hitting the wrong beat," said Agatha. "She was thrown down an old well on the allotments."

"Really? I say, what larks. Ding, dong, bell. Bull is

in the well. Come in. Don't stand glaring at me. I never liked the woman. Nasty gossip."

He led the way through the house to the garden. "Isn't there anywhere warmer?" pleaded Agatha. "It's a cold day."

"Oh, well. It's your age, you know. We'll sit in the drawing room."

"I hate you," hissed Agatha to his retreating back.

"Naughty, naughty. In here."

The drawing room was as dark as the other rooms because of the ivy covering most of the windows. Damian went around switching on lamps. A badly executed oil painting of the late Lord Bellington glared down at them. "Drink?" offered Damian.

"Not for Agatha," said Charles. "She's driving."

"One won't put me over the limit," said Agatha crossly. "Gin and tonic, please."

Charles said he would have a whisky and soda, avoiding a threatening look from Agatha.

"Now," began Agatha, "the police will be here any moment. Think! Why Mrs. Bull?"

"As I said, she was a malicious gossip. Probably nothing to do with the other murders."

"May I remind you that your sister has accused you of murdering your father?"

"Well, she would, wouldn't she?"

"Why?"

Damian brought their drinks over from an ancient sideboard. "She wants to start a farm for sick donkeys. Asked me for the money. Told her, no. She's got a large allowance. Says it's not enough. Screams and jumps up and down with rage. Does that answer your question?"

"One of them," said Agatha. "Have the police questioned Lady Bellington about Mrs. Bull's claim that she caught her down in the cellar with a syringe?"

"Over and over again. But you see, she was in a rehab in Oxford for months. And everyone down there can testify that she was not allowed to leave."

"But why would she say such a thing?" asked Charles.

"My father was toying with the idea of a reconciliation. He wrote to her. She wrote back that she would never return if Mrs. Bull was still the housekeeper. I am sure the old trout read the letter. She was always reading private correspondence."

Agatha felt herself becoming exasperated. Damian seemed perpetually amused by the whole thing. "Haven't you the faintest idea who might have murdered your father?" she demanded.

"If I had, I wouldn't have employed you. Try the villagers. They're a weird lot. People keep accusing the aristocracy of inbreeding and never take a look at these little villages, buried away from the tourist route."

"Well, give us at least a suggestion of where we should start."

"Try Mary Feathers at Lime Cottage. She's the head of the allotments committee."

But when they returned to Harby, police were going from door to door. "We'll come back in the evening," said Charles. "How are you getting on with Gerald?"

"He's a creep. He wanted me to employ him and then was lured away by Wilkes."

"I'm surprised you aren't chasing him, Agatha. You have a weakness for creeps."

"You mean men like you? Oh, let's go and eat something."

When they returned in the evening, a small moon was shining down on the huddle of houses that made up the village of Harby.

Lime Cottage was thatched, and brooded beside the village pond, its two small-paned windows at the front like two eyes. Agatha rapped on the brass knocker.

The door opened.

"Is Mrs. Feathers at home?" asked Agatha.

"I am Mrs. Feathers."

She had two wings of jet black hair tied behind her head. Her perfect face was serene and her eyes fringed with heavy lashes, wide and black. She was wearing a green cashmere sweater over a black velvet skirt.

Mrs. Feathers did not look at all like the sort of woman to head an allotment committee.

Agatha explained who they were and why they had called. "Oh, you'd better come in," she said.

She ushered them into a front parlour where a log fire was crackling cheerfully on the hearth. Three of the walls were lined with bookcases. The room was furnished with a comfortable sofa and two wing-backed chairs.

Agatha was surprised. This was hardly a horny-handed daughter of the soil. In fact, Mary's hands were soft and white.

"We want to ask you about the villagers on the al-lotments," began Agatha. Charles raised his eyebrows at her because Agatha's voice had a hectoring note. The fact was that Agatha was feeling diminished by the calm beauty in front of her. She was suddenly aware that she had not repaired her make-up and that the band of her skirt was too tight.

"I can't think of any of us who would do such a dreadful thing to Mrs. Bull," she said.

Her Gloucestershire accent was soft and caressing.

"Certainly not you," said Charles with a smile, and Agatha glared at him.

"Did Mrs. Bull have an allotment?" asked Agatha.

"No, but she would often visit and buy vegetables.

On Saturdays, various allotment holders set up stands by the road."

"Was Mrs. Bull disliked?"

"To be honest, she wasn't popular. She liked finding out nasty gossip about people."

"Where is Mr. Feathers?" asked Charles.

"I am afraid poor Roger died three years ago. Heart attack. Very sudden. But you were asking about Mrs. Bull. The trouble is that she annoyed most of the people in the village. But I cannot think of anyone who would murder her. Besides, it surely took more than one person to take her to the well and throw her down," said Gloria. "Now, Mr. Sanders at Pear Tree Cottage spends most of his time in his shed on his allotment, Charles. I mean, Sir Charles . . ."

"Charles, please."

"Well, Charles, the poor woman must have been screaming her head off."

"I've tried Mr. Sanders," said Agatha. "He slammed the door. Anyone else?"

"Let me see. Oh, I haven't offered you anything. Can I get you something?"

Charles opened his mouth to accept, but Agatha said quickly, "I'm afraid we haven't time."

"You could ask old Mrs. Ryan. Her cottage is at the back of the allotments. She may have heard something."

"Great idea!" Agatha got to her feet. "Come along, Charles."

Agatha got into the car, but Charles came round, opened the door and said, "Back in a minute. I've left something."

Oh, no, thought Agatha, watching his retreating back. He didn't leave anything. He's going to make a date with her. She peered at her face in the driving mirror. Her eyes looked tired, and there was a tiny wrinkle on her upper lip. Agatha rummaged in her bag and found she had not brought any make-up with her. Gold and red leaves danced on the road in front of the car, and a half-denuded tree raised branches up to the lowering sky as if mourning the loss of summer.

The year was dying, and with it, Agatha Raisin's hopes of ever finding a mate. Now that Gerald had walked out of her fantasies with his clay feet leaving hardly any impression on her mind, she did not even have anyone to dream about. Fickle, faithless Charles, who came and went in her life. But he was all she had left. A great wave of self-pity engulfed her. She shook herself. "Get a grip!" she snarled.

"Of what?" asked Charles, sliding into the passenger seat.

Agatha jumped nervously. "I was thinking of something and didn't hear you arrive. Did you find it?"

"Find what?"

"Don't you remember? You went back to get something."

"Oh, that. My cigarette case."

"Find it?"

"No, I must have left it at home."

"You went back there to ask her out?"

"Agatha! What if I did? It hasn't got anything to do with you, has it?"

"If it has nothing to do with me," growled Agatha, "why lie?"

"Listen! Are we going to talk to this old girl, Mrs. Ryan, or not?" demanded Charles.

Agatha opened her mouth and shut it again and drove off in the direction of the allotments.

Mrs. Ryan was a very old lady with pink scalp showing through wisps of grey hair. The skin of her face was like crumpled tissue paper, and her eyes were pale grey. She put her head on one side as Agatha and Charles introduced themselves, and then said, "Please step in to my parlour." Agatha ignored Charles's murmur of, "Said the spider to the fly," and followed her in to a dark little room where a four-bar electric heater shone a red light into the gloom. The room was crammed with upright hard chairs, spindly bamboo side tables bent under their weight of framed photographs, and a large table by the window holding sheaves of paper and a battered old Olivetti typewriter.

Mrs. Ryan looked at it and said, "I'm writing my life story. I've had a very interesting life."

Poor woman, thought Agatha cynically. Unless you're a celebrity, no one is going to want to know.

"On the night Mrs. Bull was pushed down the well," she began, "did you hear anything?"

"As a matter of fact I did. I was going to tell those policemen. They were about to come to the door, but that old bitch, Mrs. Andrews, next door, she says, 'I wouldn't bother her if I were you. She's senile.' I would like to see her face when she gets my lawyer's letter. I am suing her for defamation of character."

"Good for you," said Charles. "So what did you see?"

"Well, at first . . . Oh, can I offer you something?"

"NO!" shouted Agatha. And then said mildly, "Sorry I shouted, but I am desperate to find anything out."

"It's the menopause, dear," said the old lady. "Plays merry hell with your hormones at your age."

Warding off an explosion of wrath from Agatha, Charles said quickly, "Do tell us what you heard or saw, please."

"It must have been about four in the morning. I'm a light sleeper. I heard a *creak, creak* sort of noise from the allotments. I looked out of the window. There was this dark figure pushing a wheel barrow right up to the old well. Got the top off the well and heaved something down. I didn't know it was a body. I thought it was someone dumping their rubbish, and I meant to complain about it."

"Was there a scream or anything like that?" asked Agatha.

"No. That's why I thought it was rubbish. I meant to tell the police, and I was waiting for them to call until that fiend from hell next door told them lies about me. I didn't like to tell them anything after that because they would think, because of her slander, that I was making the whole thing up."

"Can you describe the figure of whoever it was pushing the wheelbarrow?" asked Charles.

"It was too dark. Not tall. I think he must have been wearing black clothes."

"It looks as if Mrs. Bull must have been drugged first," said Agatha. "We'll pass on your information to the police and assure them that you are perfectly sane."

"Come back anytime, particularly you, Sir Charles." She turned to Agatha, a sudden flash of malice in her old eyes. "Is he your . . . ?"

"Don't even go there," said Agatha.

Mrs. Ryan gave a little shrug. "Off you go, and let me get on with my writing."

Outside, Charles said, "She was only going to ask

you if we were an item. So why did you look at her as if you could kill her?"

But Agatha was not going to tell him that she had been sure the malicious old woman had been on the point of asking if Charles was her son, even though Charles was only six years younger than herself.

"The heat in that room was getting to me," said Agatha. "We'll drive back to the village. I'm sure Bill will be somewhere about."

In the village, they saw Bill, Wilkes, Alice, two other detectives and two policemen having a conference on the village green.

They got out of the car and went up to them. "Here comes the dynamic duo," said Wilkes. "Shove off and let us get on with some real police work."

"So you don't want to hear anything about how Mrs. Bull was drugged before she was dropped down the well?" said Agatha. "Come on, Charles."

"No! Wait!" shouted Wilkes. "What have you got?"

"Say 'pretty please,'" said Agatha.

"You tell me right now," roared Wilkes, "or I'll have you up on a charge of impeding the . . ."

"Oh, well, shut up and listen," said Agatha, and told him what they had just learned.

Wilkes listened carefully to Agatha's report and then swung round angrily to the two policemen. "Weren't you told to interview the women in those two houses next to the allotments?"

"Yes, sir. But the woman next to Mrs. Ryan said the old girl was senile."

"Is she senile?" Wilkes demanded.

"Sharp as a tack," said Charles.

"Wong and Peterson, get there immediately and take her statement."

"A thank you would be nice," said Agatha.

Wilkes turned to one of the detectives. "Blenkinsop. Take this pair into the police car and get their statements. Good day to you, Mrs. Raisin."

"Oh, fry in hell," muttered Agatha.

When their statements were taken, Agatha said, "I could murder a gin and tonic."

"No, you couldn't," said Charles. "You're driving. Take me back to Carsely. I want to go home."

"Oh, suit yourself," grumbled Agatha.

But back in Carsely when Charles had left, Agatha fought down a feeling of loneliness and compensated for it by hugging her cats. It was a pity, she thought, that she had felt obliged to give such a precious piece of information to Wilkes. But she did not have the resources of the police, and now, at the hospital, they would take samples of Mrs. Bull's blood and search for drugs.

She gave her cats a final caress and put them aside.

Something was niggling at the back of her brain. Agatha got to her feet and began to pace up and down, scowling horribly. Then her face cleared. That stone cover on the well. It had taken the use of the crowbar and all Charles's strength to break it so that the pieces could be lifted off.

She looked up Mary Feathers's phone number and rang her up. "It is late," grumbled Mary.

"I want to ask you about the covering of the well," said Agatha. "Was it a stone slab?"

"No. It was a rusty old grill. Must have been put there about early in the nineteenth century, I suppose."

Agatha thanked her and rang off. So where did that stone slab come from? Was it already lying around? Who would have the strength to drug Mrs. Bull, get her into a car, unload her onto a wheelbarrow and bring a stone slab as well?

The phone rang, the shrilling of the bell breaking into her thoughts. It was Nigel Farraday. "I've just looked at the clock," he said. "Did I wake you up?"

"No, it's all right," said Agatha.

"I was wondering if we could share a spot of dinner tomorrow evening?"

Agatha hesitated for only a moment. "Yes, that would be nice. When and where?"

"The La Vie En Rose in Mircester? French place. Just opened. Next to the George Hotel."

"Lovely. I'll be there."

When Agatha rang off, she reflected that, much as she disliked Farraday, he might come up with something else about Peta's background.

The next day was taken up by working on all the bread-and-butter stories which kept the agency going: missing teenagers, missing pets, shoplifting and divorce. Agatha decided to take a day off from the Bellington case and help her staff get through the workload.

It was only at the end of the day that Agatha realised she had no time to go home and change for dinner. And she was wearing flat-heeled boots. Even if she were meeting a man she did not much like, Agatha felt demoralised in low heels. She redid her make-up, rushed out to a nearby shoe shop and bought a pair of high-heeled black patent-leather shoes.

Nigel Farraday rose to his feet as Agatha entered the restaurant. He smoothed back his white hair and said, "You are much too glamorous to be a detective."

Agatha gave a weak smile and sat down. She surveyed the restaurant. "I haven't been here before," she remarked. The lighting was so dim she wondered if she would be able to read the menu.

"It's the latest 'in' place," said Nigel.

But to Agatha Raisin, there were no 'in' places outside London.

"What will you have as an aperitif?" asked Nigel.

"I would like a gin and tonic?"

"My dear lady," said Nigel, "the wine here is very good. You might ruin your taste buds."

Agatha ignored him and turned to the waiter and said firmly. "Yes, gin and tonic."

"I'll wait for the wine," said Nigel. "Now, dear Agatha. What would you like to eat?"

Agatha's heart sank as she read the menu. It seemed pretentious to her experienced eye. She decided to keep it simple and ordered smoked salmon to begin followed by moules marinière.

"Oh dear. That means white wine," said Nigel. "I was hoping to order a good Merlot."

"Order away," said Agatha. "I can drink red with fish."

Nigel ordered a dozen snails to be followed by steak tartare. He chose a bottle of Merlot for himself and a small decanter of the house white for Agatha.

When the waiter had left, Nigel leaned across the table. "The moment we met, I felt there was a certain je ne sais quoi between us."

"That's good," said Agatha briskly. "It means you are willing to help me find out who murdered Peta."

The look of a sulky child crossed his face. "I mean," pursued Agatha, "was she the type to make someone want to murder her?"

"Peta saw herself as a wild child," he said. "At first

93

that charmed me. But I had political ambitions, and when she turned up on the terrace at the Houses of Parliament dressed as a goth, I knew I had to get rid of her."

"Get rid of her?" echoed Agatha.

"I don't mean, 'bump her off.' I hired a private detective and found out she was being unfaithful to me, so she got nothing out of the divorce."

"Who was she having an affair with?"

"Some bit of rough who worked at some bespoke furniture business."

"Name?"

"Dear me, what a persistent lady you are. I can't remember. But the furniture place was in Camden, somewhere at the back of the market."

"What was the name of the detective agency?"

"Atkins Enquiries. Margaret Street, Oxford Circus area. Ah, here's our first course."

Agatha stared in dismay at her smoked salmon. It looked like a thin slice of raw salmon swimming in olive oil. "I didn't think any restaurant could bugger up smoked salmon," said Agatha. She summoned the waiter. "I can't eat this. Have you any soup?"

"We have cream of asparagus or minestrone."

"Take this away and bring me the minestrone," ordered Agatha.

"And don't put that salmon on the bill," said Nigel quickly.

"Don't wait for me," said Agatha. "Enjoy your snails." She remembered when she had been in France with Charles, and he had ordered snails for himself. They had been much larger than the tiny whelk-like creatures on Nigel's plate and had been swimming in garlic butter. Nigel's looked dry. When Agatha's minestrone arrived, she found it consisted of a shallow plate filled with weak broth in which floated a few vegetables. No tomatoes, no pasta, and it was lukewarm. She reminded herself sternly that she had not come for the food.

"Did Peta ever meet Lord Bellington?" she asked.

Nigel suddenly stabbed at a snail, which shot across the table into Agatha's soup.

"Oh, I am so sorry," he gabbled.

"Don't worry." Agatha fished it out and put it in an empty water glass. "Lord Bellington," she prompted.

"A few times. She flirted like mad, but then, Peta flung herself at anyone in trousers."

"Get anywhere?"

"Not after the last meeting. It was at a party in Bellington's house. Lady Bellington threw a drink in Peta's face and called her, as I remember, 'a conniving little whore' and threatened to kill her. I was gathering information for a divorce at the time, so I didn't care."

Their next course arrived. The waiter made a great fuss preparing Nigel's steak tartare, mixing it up and breaking a raw egg over it. A large pot of mussels was placed in front of Agatha. "Aren't you afraid of getting mad cow disease?" she asked Nigel. "I mean, all that raw meat?"

"'Licious," he mumbled, his mouth full. Agatha found that her mussels, subtitled on the menu as being 'Scottish rope mussels,' had not been left down in the sea for long enough. These mussels were barely out of the cradle, tiny little things. She began to feel uneasy. Nigel was drinking his bottle of wine at a great rate.

"You know, Agatha," he said. "I feel this is the start of something special."

I must nip this in the bud, thought Agatha wearily. "I felt that when Charles proposed to me," she said.

"What! You're engaged? You might have told me."

"Why on earth should I?"

"Well, for a start, why did you think I asked you out for dinner?"

Agatha sighed. "As you are a married man, I assumed you were anxious to help me with my enquiries."

His face assumed the look of a sulky, thwarted child. Agatha thought quickly. He might come in useful.

"Not that I don't find you a very attractive man," she said.

The sun visibly rose on Nigel's ego. "Can't compete with a single baronet though, can I?"

"Alas, no," smiled Agatha. She began to ask him about his life as a member of Parliament. He began to chat easily, although his voice was becoming slurred. Agatha refused any pudding, but Nigel ordered the cheese board so he had an excuse to go on drinking. He loosened his tie and took off his jacket.

At long last, after a cup of truly dreadful coffee, he called for the bill. He scanned it closely and then let out an exclamation of dismay. "I've left my wallet!"

"Oh, let me see the bill," said Agatha wearily. The restaurant was so dark that she took a small torch out of her handbag and began to scan it. "I'll powder my nose first," she said. She forgot to switch off the torch as she rose to her feet, and the light flickered on Nigel's jacket hanging on the back of his chair. That was when she saw the edge of a wallet poking out of his inside pocket. As she passed him, she reached down and took out the wallet. "Why there you are!" said Agatha, handing it to him. "Now you can relax."

When she returned, Nigel was in a bad temper. Outside the restaurant, he choked out a curt "Goodnight" and staggered off to his car.

I hope the police pull him over, thought Agatha.

As she walked round to the restaurant car park, she saw Nigel sitting in his car with the window open. He was speaking on the phone. She moved behind the shelter of a parked car and listened. "Yes, officer. Agatha

Raisin is the name. Don't know the registration but you should have it on your records. You don't need my name. I'm just a concerned citizen. These drunks have to be kept off the road."

"Snakes and bastards," muttered Agatha. "Let's see. One small carafe of wine and a gin and tonic. Better get a cab. But two can play at that game."

As another 'concerned citizen,' she waited until Nigel had driven off, having taken a note of his car registration, walked to the nearest phone box and reported him for drink driving.

Then she hailed a passing taxi and gave the driver her address.

As the cab pulled up outside her door, she saw the lights were on in her living room. Charles! It must be Charles. No one else had the code to the burglar alarm apart from her cleaner.

As she opened the door, she could hear the sound of the television set. Charles was lying on the sofa, fast asleep. She shook him awake.

"Oh, Agatha," he said. "Been out gallivanting?"

Agatha knocked his legs off the sofa and sat down next to him. "I have just endured an awful evening with Nigel Farraday in a lousy restaurant."

"What else did you expect?"

"I expected some more details on Peta. He came on to me, so I told him we were engaged."

"This is so sudden. I thought you would be experienced enough to freeze him off without lying."

"I didn't want to turn him off completely until I got some information out of him. He even tried to get me to pay for the meal by saying he had left his wallet. But I saw his wallet in his jacket and handed it to him. Was he mad! In the car park, I heard him reporting me to the police as a drunk driver, so I reported *him* and took a cab home. What an evening!"

"But did you find anything out?"

"Only that he had hired a detective agency and found she was having an affair with someone who worked in a bespoke furniture shop. I'd better go up to London tomorrow. I wouldn't bother, but I feel Peta's murder is connected to Billington's."

"I'll come with you," said Charles, stifling a yawn. "Bed, I think. Feel like giving your fiancé a good night?"

"No. We'll leave at nine."

When Charles had gone to bed, Agatha phoned Toni and gave her instructions for the following day.

Chapter Six

The next morning, Agatha and Charles left the car in a car park outside London, took the tube to Oxford Circus and walked to Margaret Street. The detective agency was above a dress shop. A small girl with pink hair and long pink nails sat in the reception area reading a film magazine which she reluctantly put down.

"We would like to see Mr. Atkins," said Agatha.

"Ain't one."

"What! Who's in charge here?"

"Mrs. Atkins, that's what."

"Are you a temp?"

"Yeah."

"I gathered that from your sod-off-don't-care atti-tude," snarled Agatha. "Tell Mrs. Atkins that Agatha Raisin and Sir Charles Fraith are here to see her. Hop to it!"

"Don't get your knickers in a twist," she mumbled and went through a frosted glass door and slammed it behind her.

The girl came out a few minutes later and held the door open. "You're to go in."

Mrs. Atkins had tinted blond hair, one of those wind-tunnel facelifts, and she was wearing a black two-piece suit with broad lapels decorated with black sequins. She was heavily made-up, and her small red-painted mouth was surrounded by a radius of wrinkles.

No ashtray, thought Agatha cheerfully. All that stuff about smoking causing wrinkles around the mouth is rubbish. Her face fell as Mrs. Atkins took a large glass ashtray out of her desk drawer and asked, "Mind if I smoke?"

"Knock yourself out," said Agatha bleakly, think-ing, I'll give up today.

"I've heard of you," said Mrs. Atkins. "So what do you want?"

"Quite a time ago you were investigating Peta Farraday. Would you still have the records?"

"That would be in my husband's time. Poor Frank died two years ago and left me the business."

"Have you got your licence?"

"Don't need it. I employ a couple of detectives who have theirs."

"So," said Agatha, "would it be possible to find records on the investigation into Peta Farraday, requested by her husband, Nigel Farraday?"

"A search will be two hundred pounds . . . cash."

Agatha bit back the angry retort that rose to her lips. "All right."

Mrs. Atkins smiled, revealing yellowish teeth stained with lipstick. "Call me Frankie. We were a pair, me and my old man: Frankie and Frank." She switched on an Apple computer on her desk. "What date?" she asked.

"I've left my iPad in the car," said Agatha.

"Never mind. The wonders of modern science. Ah, here it is. I'll just print it off for you."

Frankie seemed to be amazingly efficient although ash from her cigarette fell onto her keyboard. I must stop smoking, Agatha vowed again and for about the thousandth time. She had deliberately left her cigarettes at home. Most people these days are nauseated by the smell of cigarette smoke, but that thin line of grey smoke drifting from Frankie's cigarette wafted towards Agatha like a siren's beckoning finger.

When the printer had finished churning out the file, Frankie gathered up the papers and then said, "That will be three hundred."

"You said two hundred!" shouted Agatha.

"In fact," said Charles, "I even have it on tape."

"My mistake," said Frankie crossly. Agatha paid over the two hundred and seized the papers.

"Shabby little office," commented Agatha as they walked down the stairs. "She can't do much business."

"She must," said Charles, "to keep an address like this. Let's find a pub, have a snack and go through these papers."

But a thin cold rain was falling, and the lunchtime pubs were busier than usual. "I'll try the Ivy," said Agatha, taking out her phone.

"At this late date?" protested Charles. "They only take celebrities."

"Watch and listen," said Agatha.

"This is Penelope Bryce-Sandringham of *Tatler*," Charles heard Agatha cooing into the phone. "I'm secretary to our new restaurant reviewer, Agatha Raisin. She would be most grateful if you had an available table for, say, one o'clock. Yes, I'll wait. Oh good. Splendid!"

Agatha rang off and hailed a taxi.

In the expensive quiet of one of London's most

famous restaurants, Agatha ordered a gin and tonic and began to read the notes, passing each page to Charles after she had finished, only breaking off to order food. The restaurant prided itself on traditional British cooking. They decided to skip the starters and both ordered steak and kidney pie.

The food was so good that they put aside the notes to eat, only going back to them over coffee.

"Right," said Agatha. "The furniture man is called Toby Cross. I've got the home address and the address in Camden Town of the furniture place. It's called You Would, Wood You? There's also a Peter Welling, Harlestone Place, Kensington. No mention of work. He was knocking her off as well."

"Dear Agatha," murmured Charles. "Always the romantic."

"We'll try the Camden address first."

Agatha had envisaged a large workshop, open to the street and smelling of wood, but You Would, Wood You? had a shopfront with a plate glass window displaying one Sheraton-type chair with a drape of blue velvet over one arm.

A young man was seated behind a Regency table which served as a reception desk. On the table was a phone of the old-fashioned type where you talk into it and hold the other bit to your ear. It was in white and gold vulcanite.

The young man rose to meet them. "How can I be of assistance?" he asked in a public school accent.

Agatha quickly summed him up, from his mop of curls to his square face and broad figure clad in an oatmeal sweater and plum-coloured cords, as a "posh rugger-bugger."

"Have you still got a chap called Toby Cross working for you?" asked Agatha.

"Would you like to order some shelves or something?" he asked wistfully. "I'd like to justify my existence."

"Surely they don't expect you to go on like a double glazing salesman?" asked Agatha, momentarily diverted. "I mean, they can't expect you to *push* bespoke furniture, can they?"

"My father knows old Bonlieu who owns this business. So he gives me this job because he says they haven't time to teach me woodworking."

"So why don't you pack it in?" asked Charles.

"Because Pa says he'll disinherit me if I lose this one like I did all the others."

"But why . . . ?" began Agatha, but Charles said firmly, "Toby Cross."

"Okay. Follow me. I'm Jake Lisle."

"Agatha Raisin and Charles Fraith."

So they followed him through a door at the back of reception and found themselves in a huge workplace, full of the sound of sawing and planing. "He's got his area at the back," yelled Jake. "I can't see him, but he's probably brewing up tea in his cubbyhole." He pointed off to a small partitioned area at the back of the shop. "Wait here. I'll go in and get him." He pushed open the flimsy door.

They waited. "What's up with the boy?" complained Agatha.

She and Charles pushed open the door and then stood, frozen with horror. Jake was standing there, holding a bloody severed head. The young man's face was greenish-white, and he looked ready to faint. Later, Agatha thought if she had not been so concerned to preserve the crime scene, she might have fainted herself.

"Put the head down where you got it," she shouted, "and walk away."

Numbly, and as if sleepwalking, Jake put the horrible head on a small table littered with tools. The decapitated body was sitting in a battered armchair, and the flimsy wooden walls of the cubbyhole were drenched in blood.

"Get the police, Charles," said Agatha. "I'll try to help Jake. Then see if you can get someone in charge to cordon off the area."

A man walked up to Agatha. "What's up with him?"

"Toby Cross has been murdered," said Agatha. "We're waiting for the police. Can someone get this boy tea or brandy?"

A man who seemed to be the manager joined them and listened in horror to Agatha's discovery. He started shouting out orders. Soon, the cubbyhole was fenced off with lengths of wood. Jake was given brandy, and some colour began to return to his cheeks.

"It's a joke, isn't it?" he pleaded.

"Don't think so," said Agatha.

"I thought it was, you see. That's why I picked up the head. I was going to carry it out and bowl it at them, and then I saw my hands were sticky with blood and . . . and . . . there was this smell of shit and blood and . . ."

"There, now," said Agatha. "Have another swig of brandy. Here comes a nice policeman."

" 'To put you to bed, and here comes a chopper to chop off your head,' " murmured Charles behind Agatha, making her jump.

"What a long day," sighed Agatha. Detectives had followed police and then a forensic team, photographer, pathologist had arrived. She and Charles gave long interviews until Agatha felt she could scream.

As they left the police station, they saw the dejected figure of Jake sitting on the steps. "I thought you would be in hospital being treated for shock," exclaimed Agatha.

"It's awful. Pa arrived with Mr. Bonlieu and Bonlieu said he would have to fire me. He said I had been a disaster. He got to hear I had told some customers that maybe they'd be better off at Ikea. So Pa says it's either the army or I get out and make my own way."

"You'd better come back with us. I'll find you work," said Agatha.

Charles groaned.

"But first," went on Agatha, "I think we should book into some hotel. I've got to try to see that other chap in Kensington tomorrow."

After a fortifying all-day breakfast, Agatha said to Jake, "Feel like talking a bit about it? The police wouldn't tell me anything. Didn't they offer you victim support?"

"Yes, but then Pa turned up and all I wanted to do was get away from him."

"What about your mother?"

"Dead."

"Oh, sorry. But before the questions, don't you want to go home and pack some things?"

"And get shouted at? I'll wash out my smalls tonight. What do you want to know?"

"Why did no one hear him screaming?"

"Well, there's always a lot of noise."

"Was he allowed to take a break when he felt like it?" asked Charles.

"He was one of the few independent craftsmen. He could do chairs that looked like Chippendale or Sheraton. Great favourite with the new rich. He could make his own hours just so long as he delivered the finished product on time."

"When you picked up the head, was the blood wet or tacky?" asked Agatha.

"The police asked me that. It must have been sort of sticky. I got the stuff on my hands. That's why I thought at first it was a joke until I saw the rest of the body."

"Did anyone see him at all today? I mean, when we asked, you said he was in his cubbyhole. How did you know?"

"One of his clients came in early and asked to see him. Toby led the man into his office."

"But how did you know he was still there?" pursued Agatha.

"Because one of the fellows going out for lunch said, 'Toby stays in that hole of his all day. When does he work?'"

"I said he had keys to the place and sometimes worked all night."

Agatha stared at him for a long moment. Then she said slowly, "When each chair was finished, was it then sent to an upholsterer?"

"No, Toby did that as well after the client had chosen the right sort of cloth, usually Regency stripes or something dead unimaginative like that."

"Drugs!" exclaimed Agatha.

"In the chairs?" said Charles. "If the man was peddling drugs, he could carry them easier in his pocket."

"*A lot* of drugs," said Agatha stubbornly.

"Forget it. I'm tired." Charles stifled a yawn.

But Agatha's eyes were gleaming. "You don't have any keys to the warehouse, Jake?"

"Oh, lor', yes. I forgot to give them back. But if you're thinking of going there, the police will be all over the place."

"They'll have gone by now," said Agatha.

"But there'll be police tape on the doors."

"Not all of the doors! Is there one at the back?"

"Yes, but . . ."

"Let's go," said Agatha excitedly.

"If were given to sulk, I would sulk," said Charles bitterly. "Oh, I suppose I'd better join you, if only to watch you making a fool of yourself."

They stopped the taxi a good bit away from the premises and then Jake led them to the back of the property by a circuitous route. He fished in his briefcase and brought out a ring of keys.

"Switch on the lights," said Agatha.

"That'll bring the police!" exclaimed Jake.

"If we walk about flashing torches, someone's more likely to get suspicious," said Agatha. "If they see all the lights blazing, they'll think it has something to do with the work."

"What! With police tape on the front door?" said Charles.

"I didn't see any police tape," snarled Agatha. She flicked a torch round the walls, located a bank of light switches and turned several on.

"Is there any point in telling you that the front of the building is probably taped off?" said Charles.

Agatha ignored him. "Lead the way, Jake. I don't want to muck up the crime scene. If Toby had any chairs ready for delivery, where would they be?"

"Through that door on the left. That leads to the storeroom. Beyond that is the garage. If he's got any stuff, it'll be easy to find. He's got his own label. Become quite famous has Toby."

"Oh, Aggie," said Charles. "Let's get to bed. If he had become a famous furniture maker, then it stands to reason he wouldn't need more money out of anything illegal."

But Agatha opened the door to the storeroom and switched on the overhead fluorescent lights.

"The last commission he had was for a set of dining chairs for the Malimbian Embassy," said Jake. "I suppose those crates in the corner are the chairs. They've got Toby's name on them."

"Okay, Jake," said Agatha. "There's a crowbar. Open up one of them."

Charles waited for Jake to protest, but Jake was in the grip of a new freedom offered by this odd woman who had offered him accommodation and a job. He no longer had to fear his father. He cheerfully seized the crowbar and prised open a side of the crate. Four chairs were wrapped and stacked.

"Lift out one of the chairs and slit open the upholstery," said Agatha.

"You're not wearing gloves. Your fingerprints will be all over the place, and you will be charged with wanton vandalism," said Charles.

"There's no need to slit the upholstery at the top. Maybe we can get in through the bottom," said Jake. "I'll fetch some carpentry tools."

"Good lad. Go to it."

When Jake returned, he made a little opening and poked and prodded with a chisel, but there seemed to be nothing but stuffing.

Agatha saw the cynical, amused look on Charles's face and suddenly realised the enormity of what she had encouraged Jake to do.

"Wrap it up again," she urged. "And then we'd better wipe our fingerprints off."

"That's odd," said Jake.

"What's odd?" demanded Agatha. "Oh, hurry up. I must have been mad."

"The balance," said Jake. "It seems as if one leg's heavier than the other. Well, in for a penny, in for a pound." And as Agatha and Charles wailed, "Noooooo!" Jake seized a saw and began to saw the leg off. The leg of the chair fell to the floor, and out of it rolled what looked like gravel.

"There you are," said Agatha. "It's only some stuff to add weight."

Charles knelt down and picked up what looked like a grey pebble. "Uncut diamonds," he said.

"Police!" shouted a voice from the doorway.

A uniformed policeman strode in followed by a short, burly looking man with a red face.

"Oh, God!" said Agatha.

"Worse than God," said Jake. "It's Pa."

"It's alright officer," said Mr. Lisle. "That's my son. He's not right in the head. Don't phone it in. No charges."

"You'd better phone it in, officer," said Jake triumphantly. "We've found uncut diamonds in the leg of this chair."

Charles took out his phone. "I'm calling my lawyer," he said.

Agatha had suffered long interviews with the police

before, but this latest round of grillings left her close to exhausted tears. First there was the local police and detectives. Then came detectives from Scotland Yard, followed later by Special Branch and after them, three quiet men in well-tailored suits and with hard eyes.

"I am not a racist!" Agatha had howled at one time. How could she explain this odd intuition of hers? They assumed, because it was an African Embassy, she had suspected villainy. While the long interrogations went on, they were moved to Paddington Green station and allowed only a few hours' sleep.

After two days and with warnings not to leave the country, they were let out and allowed to go home.

It was a brisk cold sunny day as the three of them stood like owls on the steps of Paddington Green station, blinking in the sunlight, having said goodbye to their respective lawyers.

They were just about to hail a taxi when a limousine drove up. "Pa," said Jake.

"My boy," said Mr. Lisle, bounding up the steps, "I have secured a place for you at Sandhurst."

"I've got a job," said Jake. "Honest. I'd make a lousy soldier. This lady has hired me as a detective."

Agatha supressed a groan. She had planned to find employment like gardening for Jake until he found something in line with his mental abilities like, maybe, construction work.

"Then she's as big a fool as you are. May you rot. I'll send your stuff on." He glared at Agatha. "What's your address?"

Had Agatha not been so exhausted, she would have yelled at Mr. Lisle and then told him to take his son away. But she only wanted to get to bed, and Jake was looking at her like a whipped puppy.

She handed over her card and said mildly, "Shove off. Taxi!"

The three dived into a cab with the raging voice to Jake's father ringing in their ears. "Let's get back to the hotel and pay the bill and get home," said Agatha. "Oh, my cats! They wouldn't let me phone Doris." Doris Simpson, Agatha's cleaner, often looked after the cats while Agatha was away. "I'll phone her now and say I'll be home as soon as possible."

"Agatha!" protested Charles. "Not one of us is fit to drive."

"I am," said Jake.

Charles grinned. "Doesn't the boy make you feel old, Aggie?"

But Agatha was busy phoning Doris.

Back at last in Carsely, all of them feeling grubby and exhausted. Charles collected his own car and left for his home. Agatha wearily showed Jake the spare room but said she would use the bathroom first. When she finally emerged, clean and ready for bed, she went into the spare bedroom to tell Jake he could use the bathroom, but he was fast asleep, sprawled across the top of the bed. She decided to leave him as he was.

Agatha awoke late. She squinted at the clock. It was after ten. She struggled into her clothes and went downstairs to a welcome from her cats and the smell of fresh coffee.

Doris Simpson, her cleaner, was working in the kitchen. "Sit down, love," said Doris, "and I'll get you a mug of coffee. You're in the newspapers. I bought them all at the shop. They're on the table."

"What are they saying?" asked Agatha.

"Just that you and Sir Charles had been taken to Paddington Green for enquiries."

"Oh, snakes and bastards. That's where they take terrorists. Doris, I've got a young man upstairs."

"Well, you know me, Agatha. I never was a one to judge. They say these here winter summer . . ."

"I am not having an affair," howled Agatha. "But he's going to work for me, and he needs clothes. Could you be an angel and go to Marks in Mircester and see if you can buy him stuff to be going on with? I'll give you plenty of money, and take enough as well to pay for your time . . . and petrol, of course."

Doris took down Agatha's little used sewing basket from a cupboard and fished out a measuring tape. "I'll best measure the lad."

Because of all the dramas he had been through, when Jake awoke to find a white-haired lady measuring him, his first mad idea was that he was being sized up for a coffin, and jumped out of bed with a yell.

Doris rapidly explained things. She opened a wardrobe and handed Jake one of Charles's dressing gowns and suggested he wash, and leave all his dirty clothes on the bed so that she could put them in the washing machine.

When Jake finally erupted into the kitchen, all shining-morning-face, Agatha winced and felt her age.

"So when do we get started?" he asked eagerly.

"First," said Agatha, "we find you a flat, and then I'll think up some work to keep you going until you find a proper job."

He looked almost ludicrous in his dismay. "But I thought I was going to be a detective!"

"But you have no training. And you can't be a detective until you get a certificate."

"You could take me on as a trainee," pleaded Jake.

The phone rang. "Answer that, Jake," said Agatha. "If it's the press, I'll talk to them later. Oh, and if it is someone called Roy Silver, I am out detecting."

It was Roy Silver. "He always wants to come and visit when he thinks there is a chance of getting some publicity for himself," explained Agatha. "I'm very fond of him, but if he wants to come this week-end, I don't feel up to it. Tell him I'm up in London somewhere." Jake conveyed the message.

The doorbell shrilled. "I'll get it," said Jake.

A tall, handsome man stood on the doorstep. "Who are you?" he demanded sharply.

"I'm Agatha's latest . . ."

He had been about to say, "detective," but the angry man made a sound of disgust and strode off.

"Who was it?" asked Agatha.

"Big chap. Asked who I was. I started to say I was your latest detective, but I only got as far as latest when he stormed off."

"Oh, dear. I've a feeling that was my ex. He lives next door. We'll wait here until Doris comes back with clothes for you. You can pay me back when you get work. I'll need to buy you a cheap car."

In the early evening, Agatha introduced Jake to her staff, who always reported back before going their separate ways. "He is a trainee," said Agatha. "He can start off by going out with one of you and observing how it's done. Simon, you've got that supermarket job. Take Jake with you tomorrow."

Simon noticed the way that Jake kept looking at Toni. Although he had persuaded himself he was no longer interested in Toni, he didn't want to see anyone else snatching her away.

"What do we have to do?" asked Jake.

"We keep an eye out for shoplifters."

"But supermarkets usually have a security guard," said Jake.

"This one has. But he's an ex-copper and due to retire in a couple of days' time, and they don't want to spoil his leave-taking by accusing him of incompetence. He's been very good up until recently when his sight began to fail."

Agatha had been busy that day. She had found Jake a studio flat near the office and had bought him a cheap secondhand car. She brushed aside his thanks, saying that he could pay her off when he found a proper job. She was glad to say goodnight to him. Agatha did not want to be seen around with a handsome young man. She had a cynical feeling that people would not think Jake her toy boy, but more likely, her son. The company of youth, thought Agatha sadly, can be very lowering, bringing on feeling of "been there, done that, felt that, yawn."

Jake said he would brave a confrontation with his father in order to get his clothes and things from home.

When Agatha returned, she found both James and Charles waiting for her. "Oh, feel free to use my house any time you just want to walk in," snarled Agatha. "Get me a drink, and then tell me why you are both here."

Charles fixed her a gin and tonic, and then sat down

next to her on the sofa while James stood in front of the fireplace and looked solemnly at her.

"It never works out, you know," said James.

Agatha glared at Charles. "Didn't you tell him that I have no interest either maternal or sexual in that young man?"

"No, I didn't," said Charles. "You are always making a fool of yourself over one man or another. Why not this one?"

"Don't be so stupid!" raged Agatha. "He found those diamonds. Maybe there is some connection to Peta. I couldn't just abandon him. He wants to be a detective, so he's working as a trainee. Simon can look after him. I've got to go back to London to see that other man, Peter Welling."

"Oh, hell," said Charles. "I suppose I had better go with you. But haven't you noticed how very good-looking young Jake is? And didn't you have enough of good-looking men recently when one tried to murder you? Wonder what Toni will make of him."

"I would go with you," said James, "but I have a plane to catch in the morning. Don't do anything stupid, Agatha."

"Of course she will," said Charles cheerfully. "She's not going to change to suit you!"

In the morning, before she left for London with Charles, Agatha took a good look at young Jake. He had thick curly black hair, large hazel eyes fringed with thick sooty lashes, a square handsome face and a strong body with very long legs. Agatha noticed Jake had said something to make Toni laugh, and Simon was looking like thunder. Although Simon was still pursuing Alice, he did not want anyone to succeed with Toni where he had failed. Bill Wong had found a flat in the same block as Alice, and that was making Simon's pursuit of her even more difficult.

The supermarket was within walking distance. As Simon and Jake strolled along, Jake asked, "Has the beautiful Toni got a fellow?"

"No," said Simon, deciding to lie. "She's a lesbian."

"What a waste," said Jake. "What about Agatha?"

"Come on. She's old enough to be your granny."

"Maybe. Very sexy. Have you noticed her legs?"

"Oh, shut up. We've got work to do."

Peter Welling turned out to live in a pretty white stuccoed house in Kensington. "Mistress area," commented Charles. "Back in early Victorian times, they put the other woman out here. Far enough from London then to be discreet."

Agatha suddenly had a weak hope that Peter would turn out to have left this address or gone abroad or anything to stop her for having to conduct another interview. It was all too complicated. If she had been paid to investigate Peta's murder, that would have been straightforward. But there was the case of Lord Bellington and then Mrs. Bull. Was Mrs. Bull alive? Had she been able to identify her attacker? If that were the case, then her case and the case of Lord Bellington could both have been solved. She stood with her hand on the garden gate and with her mouth open.

"Are you going to stand there in la-la land?" demanded Charles.

Agatha gave herself a mental shake. "Remind me again why I am wasting time on Peta's murder."

"Because you felt there was a connection."

"Oh, right. You know, Charles. I'm suddenly weary I want a fire and . . . and muffins, and slippers, and . . ."

"You want escape. Don't we all," said Charles. "Let's get on with nasty reality."

He rang the bell beside the black lacquered door. An old wisteria, devoid of its leaves, surrounded the door like withered, clutching hands.

The door was opened by a maid, a tall figure in black dress, white cap and white apron.

Charles introduced them and asked if it were possible to see Mr. Welling. The maid held open the door to a drawing room, which ran from front to back of the house, and told them to wait.

"Odd," whispered Agatha. "I didn't think anyon had a parlourmaid anymore. It's like finding yours in the middle of a costume drama."

The door was held open and a tall grey-haired figure swept in wearing a long lace gown and carrying a glass walking stick.

"We hoped to speak to Mr. Welling," said Agatha.

"I am he. I think tea would be nice. Jeremy. Tea."

Jeremy bobbed a curtsey and went out. Two transvestites, marvelled Agatha.

"Mr. Welling . . ."

"Do call me Peter."

"We are investigating the murder of Peta Currie," said Agatha. "I believe you knew her."

"Oh, Peta. What larks we had. Mind you, when I read about her murder, I was not surprised."

"Why?" asked Charles.

"She wasn't above a bit of blackmail, sweetie, and so I tell you. You see, my parents were still alive, and if they had known I was a trannie, I would have been disinherited, and this house and all the spondulicks would have gone to creepy cousin Alwin. Peta was fun. She wanted an escort she didn't have to go to bed with for a change, and I wanted a glamour puss to show to the parents. Well, one evening she ups and demands money or says she will go to the parents and tell them, and she's sneaked the photos to show them. I could have strangled the bitch. I mean all I had was a small allowance from a trust and a mews house. She says to sell the mews. So I hold her off by saying I've put it on the market. Then the parents died in that Paris air crash, so I told her to say anything she wanted. I'd never thought of killing anyone before, but I used to lie awake at night and dream of ways to kill Peta. When I read about her murder, I wondered what poor bastard she had driven to do it.

"Ah, tea and muffins. Splendid. And put a match to the logs, Jeremy. It's a teensy bit cold in here."

Charles wondered uneasily if Agatha were psychic. The only things missing were the slippers put on the hearth to warm.

"You may join us, Jeremy," said Peter, inclining his head.

"Ever so kind, I'm sure, mum," said Jeremy. "I'll serve first."

They were indeed like a pair out of a costume drama, thought Agatha. Peter had a high-nosed aristocratic face, and Jeremy had the harsh plain looks of a down-trodden class.

Charles asked, "Did Peta ever say anything about anyone wanting to kill her husband?"

"Not that I can recall. I read a lot about it in the newspapers. Someone murdering Peta, now, that I can understand. Bellington? I am sure there is no connection. In these cases, it is always about money. Cherchez le dosh, as I always say."

Agatha suddenly felt claustrophobic. The room, like

its occupants, was designed to fit the period. The mantle over the fireplace was draped with gold silk. Stuffed birds in glass cases stood on little side tables. Antimacassars decorated the backs of the sofa and easy chairs.

"I am afraid we must go," she said firmly, refusing a buttered muffin.

"Call again," said Peter grandly. "Jeremy, show them out."

"You know," said Agatha when they headed for the tube to take them out to where the car was parked, "when I worked in London, I wouldn't have been taken back or surprised by that pair. I've become countrified."

"Too right," said Charles amiably, "Nothing like down-to-earth poisons and chucking people down wells."

Agatha stopped short in the Gloucester Road. "I must phone Patrick. Maybe Mrs. Bull has told them who tried to kill her."

Charles waited while Agatha talked urgently into her phone. When she had rung off, she said, "Mrs. Bull says she bought a bottle of beer from the local shop, drank it, and that's the last she remembered until the pain of being chucked down the well. Once the grill had been wrenched off the top, it seems that slab was propped to one side and could easily have been levered up and onto the top."

"But if someone drugged her beer, it must have been someone who called at her home," said Charles.

"She says no one called, but the police think she may be too frightened to mention any name. I now wonder if that business with the diamonds has anything to do with the murders. Patrick said it's all gone hush-hush."

"Oh, the dark corridors of power will be diplomatically sorting that out. But they'll need to produce a murderer because it's been all over the newspapers. I've just thought of something, Aggie. What do we know about Gerald? We know he worked for Scotland Yard, but that doesn't make him a saint. What if Peta had something on him? Maybe she knew him from her days in London? And why settle in the Cotswolds?"

"I've been interviewed by detectives from Scotland Yard before, including this last lot," said Agatha, "and I can't think of even one who was in any way friendly. Signed the official secrets act and threatened. I know the crime reporter of the *Sketch*. Let's go and see him. Taxi!"

Agatha phoned from the taxi and found that Alex Cameron, the crime reporter, was drinking in El Vino's, that favourite watering hole of journalists in Fleet Street.

He was on his own, sitting at a table with a bottle of wine in front of him. He was a squat, paunchy man with a face criss-crossed with little red broken veins, a loose mouth, and dyed-brown hair combed over a freckled scalp.

They sat down at his table, and he eyed them blearily. "Fleet Street's not the same since all the newspapers left," he said. "This is the last bit of it. If you want a drink, buy your own."

"Just a bit of info," said Agatha. "Ever hear of a detective inspector called Gerald Devere?"

"Something there. Need to get back to the old files. Can't be bothered."

"I'm officially investigating Lord Bellington's murder," said Agatha. "You help me, and I'll make sure you'll get an exclusive."

"Now, you're talking. Let's go."

Agatha was amazed at the seemingly small number of staff in the offices of the *Sketch* and commented on it. "Not like the old days," said Alex. "Most done by agencies and freelancers. I'm for the chop soon. I know it. Got me a cubicle. Can't call it an office. Squeeze in."

"Don't you keep everything on a computer?" marvelled Agatha as the old reporter scrabbled in a large filing cabinet. "Could never get used to the things," he grumbled. "I'm a paper man, me. Ah, here we are. I 'member him now. Had to give that one backhanders for every bit of information."

He heaved his bulk onto a small typing chair and

opened a dusty file. "Ah, knew there was something. You heard of Mad Max?"

"The gangster. Yes. Found shot in his garden five years ago."

"I was on that. His missus, Gloria, claimed Devere raped her. Hell of a scandal. Finally hushed up. Devere resigned but with an honourable discharge as they say in the army. Wouldn't have got away with it now with all this new puritanism."

"I wouldn't call all these recent allegations of sexual harassment puritanism," said Agatha.

"Well, you wouldn't. Bloody women!"

"Run me off a copy," said Agatha, "and get me Gloria's current address, and, yes, I'll remember you when the story breaks."

"You'd better."

Mad Max Harrison's wife lived in a flat in Chelsea Harbour. "It's very quiet here," commented Agatha, "and most of the apartments look empty."

"I heard somewhere that very rich foreigners buy them as investments," said Charles. "It's been an odd day so far. It wouldn't surprise me in the least to find that Gloria has turned into a fellow. How did you get to know a crime reporter? Surely in your PR days, you dealt with fashion editors and so on."

"My first client ever was a murder suspect," said Agatha. "Oh, here we are. I'll tell you about it someday. Thank goodness, the woman's on the ground floor. Do you ever watch the Montalbano series on television? I always want to book a holiday in Sicily every time I watch it, but then Inspector Montalbano always seems to be running up and down steep steps and my legs ache just . . ."

"Agatha! Stop babbling and ring the bloody woman's bell."

She ran the doorbell, which chimed out the theme from *The Godfather*. Agatha had envisaged a stereotype of a gangster's wife: leopard-print top, backless mules, face paint so thick you could skate on it and dead black hair scraped up on top of her head. So Gloria, who looked pretty much like that, came as no surprise.

But her voice was. In a glacial upper-class voice, Gloria demanded, "Who are you and what do you want?"

Agatha introduced them and explained they were investigating the background of Gerald Devere.

"You'd better come in," she said. "The salon's through here."

The salon, as she had called it, had been designed by a soulless expert. No curtains. White linen blinds at the window. White nubbly material sofa and armchairs. Glass-topped coffee table. A huge stone vase of autumn leaves, dipped in glycerine to preserve them, stood in front of the empty grey stone hearth. Weak sunlight shone on the marina outside where yachts bobbed at anchor. Little sunlight waves flickered across the ceiling.

She ordered them to sit down and asked, "What do you want to know about Gerald? It's all old hat."

"We have learned," said Agatha, "that you accused him of raping you."

"So what's that got to do with anything?" asked Gloria. She had a heavy pendulous face and thick-lidded eyes.

"We're investigating the murder of a woman in the village of Carsely, where Mr. Devere has just moved to. If he did indeed rape you, then it follows that he's capable of violence."

"Get your drift." Gloria lit a cigarette. "Fact is, he was set up. Max wanted him to stop snooping around, and Gerald had this reputation for being after anything in a skirt. So I was told to come on to him, and the minute he got my knickers off, to start yelling rape. Well, Gerald got off the charge, and Max was furious because he had told me to get him to rough me up first and so there was no real evidence. But Gerald had such a reputation with the ladies that his bosses never quite believed him, so Max got rid of him after all."

"So Gerald was not capable of being violent?"

"Don't think so. But Max used to say a lot of coppers become like villains, know what I mean?" Traces of a Cockney accent were beginning to show through.

"It's very quiet here," said Charles. "I would have thought you would have preferred somewhere livelier."

"Billy likes it. He likes a bit o' posh. Here! I'm forgetting, he'll be home soon. I wear my own sort of clothes when he's not around, but I'd better change. Can you stay a bit? You're a 'Sir.' He'll be ever so pleased to find a sir here. The bar's through that door over by the windows. Help yourselves." She hurried out of the room.

"I'm going to have a gin and a cigarette," said Agatha. "What a weird day."

"I'll join you," said Charles. "When in Looking-Glass Country, always fortify yourself. What do you think Billy will be like?"

"Probably another gangster or used car dealer," said Agatha. "What a well-stocked bar!"

Just as they were carrying their drinks back into the salon, they heard the scrape of a key in the front door. "Billy," whispered Agatha. "Wonder what he's like?"

Billy walked into the room. He came as a surprise. He was a small fussy man dressed in pinstriped trousers and a dark jacket, striped shirt and silk tie. He was about fifty or so: thick grey hair, sharp nose, small mouth and eyes.

Charles and Agatha explained who they were and why they had called. "Ah, Max," said Billy. "Used to be a client of mine down at the Old Bailey."

"You are a barrister!" exclaimed Agatha.

"William Baxter, ma'am. All sorts of villains defended. So you want to know about Devere? I wouldn't mind having been on the prosecution for that one, but I'm strictly defence."

Gloria came quietly back into the room. She was wearing a pale blue cashmere twinset over a tweed skirt. She had loosened her hair and tied it back with a thin velvet ribbon.

"Get me a drink," ordered Billy. "The usual. Hop to it."

"Yes, dear."

"I heard about Gerald. Nothing unsavoury except a habit of seducing his fellow officers' wives. Max was always as thick as pig shit, and if Gerald had kept it in his pants, he would have kept his job as well."

Gloria came back with Billy's drink on a little silver tray. "Nuts!" he barked. "Where are the nuts?"

"Right away." Gloria scuttled off, head bent, figure slightly to the side, reminding Charles of a geisha.

When Gloria came back with a bowl of nuts, Charles and Agatha decided to leave. At the front door, Agatha whispered to Gloria, who had been ordered to see them out, "You have my card. I can help in divorces."

"We aren't married."

"Then walk, girl!"

"Whatever do you mean?"

"Gloria!" came Billy's peremptory voice.

"Gotta go," she said.

Outside, a blustery wind was rocking the boats in the marina. "Why?" asked Agatha.

"Oh, I don't know," said Charles. "Maybe it's the same as getting a bride from the Philippines or the Ukraine. Looking for the old-fashioned idea of the domestic slave. I guess some villains' wives have to be like that."

"What a day!" said Agatha. "Thank goodness there aren't so many weirdos in the country."

"You mean all those people bumping each other off is normal?"

Back in Carsely, Agatha was overtaken by a desire to beg Charles to stay the night. But he pecked her on the cheek and scampered off to his own car before she could summon up the courage. She told herself it was a relief, that she was not into casual sex, although a jeering voice said, "Oh, really? These days, you're not into sex at all!"

She went in and let her cats out into the garden. The doorbell rang. It was Jake. "Mind if I have a word," he said.

"Come in. I could do with a coffee. What about you?"

"Fine."

Agatha switched the electric kettle and spooned instant coffee into two mugs.

"So what's your problem?" she asked. "I gather you do have a problem."

"It's this supermarket job with Simon. I caught two shoplifters today, and on each occasion when I was about to march them up to the manager's office, Simon said, 'You stay on lookout.' When we were finishing for the day, the manager shook Simon's hand and said, 'Well done, young man.' Simon gave me no credit whatsoever."

Agatha put a cup of coffee down in front of Jake. "Simon had a thing for Toni, and although I believe it's over, he will still be jealous of you and not want you to get the kudos for anything. I should have thought of that. I'll give you something to start doing on your own tomorrow. Okay?"

"Thanks. How did you get on today?"

Agatha began to describe her adventures, and Jake began to laugh and laugh until Agatha joined in. "It was all so weird," said Agatha. "First the transvestites and then the villain's missus."

Then Agatha asked him why he had failed at so many previous jobs. "I was a bit of a rebel, but then, Pa is very controlling. I got a good second in English Literature, but, I mean, that doesn't qualify you for a job, so I said I was going to be an apprentice plumber and learn the trade, and Pa hit the roof. I said plumbers made a lot of money, and I wanted my own money. He bullied me into several jobs in businesses belonging to his friends, and like a spoilt brat I just behaved as badly as possible until they sacked me. I think I could be good at this detective job, but not with Simon."

"I'll put you with Toni tomorrow. Don't get any ideas there."

"I won't. But why?"

"Talking about controlling parents," said Agatha with a sigh. "I suppose I look on Toni as a daughter, and I don't want to see her getting hurt. Now, have you eaten?"

"No."

"We'll go to the White Hart Royal in Moreton. They do a very good lamb and mint pie."

Mr. and Mrs. Ian Frimp were new to the village of Carsely. They were dining that evening in the White Hart Royal. Ruby Frimp scowled over her menu at Agatha. "There's that detective woman," she whispered. "She flirting with a *boy!*"

"Good luck to her," said her husband.

"But she's corrupting a minor!"

That made her husband put down his menu and take

a look. "Ruby, that chap is in his late twenties, I should guess, and good luck to the woman. Now, choose something to eat and shut up. It was your idea to move from Manchester to this living grave. No one bothers about the neighbours in Manchester. But all you do is poke and pry."

"The vicar's wife shall hear about this," muttered Ruby.

Agatha and Jake were enjoying each other's company enormously. They drank two bottles of wine. Jake began to think Agatha was the sexiest thing on two legs he had seen in a long time.

They decided to take a taxi to Carsely because they were over the limit. In the taxi, Jake put an arm around Agatha and kissed her on the cheek. Agatha fought down her rising conscience. What had she got to feel guilty about? She was free. He was free. Okay, she was a bit older. Years older, screamed her conscience. Agatha's conscience and hormones joined in the battlefield of her mind, and her hormones won. Then she began to take inventory. Her legs were shaved. But should she have had a Brazilian? Nope. They said that men who liked women shaved down there were latent paedophiles.

As the taxi drew up outside Agatha's cottage, she saw with a feeling of acute disappointment mixed with relief that the lights were on in the living room.

"We've got company," she said. "Charles is here, which means the spare room will be occupied. You'll need to sleep on the couch."

"Suits me," said Jake. "Then I'll drive you down in the morning to pick up your car."

Charles rose to meet them. He had been at a dinner party at a mansion nearby and had decided to drop in on Agatha on his road home. But one look at the tipsy pair made him decide to stay. There was nothing for Agatha in an affair with that young man but hurt, he thought.

Agatha walked slowly into the kitchen in the morning with a sore head and a mouth like a gorilla's armpit. Jake rose to meet her. "I've collected your car," he said. "So we can get started."

"Not without coffee."

"You're late," said Jake. "I put some in a thermos. You can drink it at the office. I'll drive you in your car."

"Okay," said Agatha weakly. "I didn't know it was so late."

"Don't worry. With me driving, we'll be there on time."

How could I ever be mad enough to even think about ~ing to bed with this young man, thought Agatha. I ~ a hundred this morning.

In the office, as she was beginning to send her staff off on their respective jobs, she had a sudden idea. "Toni. I would like you and Jake here to go back to Harby Hall and then to the village. See if there is anything at all you can find out. Toni, you'll need to use your car. Jake's is at my place." Then Agatha found to her fury that she was blushing.

Chapter Seven

Simon went off to the supermarket, seething with rage. Harby Hall was the prime investigation. This upstart newcomer, Jake, should not have been allowed anywhere near it. Also, it was being forcefully borne in on Simon that his pursuit of Alice was beginning to make him look ridiculous. And so his thoughts turned to Toni again. She had been looking particularly pretty that morning in a cherry red sweater.

Jake was happily thinking the same thing as he sat next to Toni in her small car. It was a bright sunny day with the colourful leaves of autumn dancing in front of them on the country roads.

"I had a marvellous evening out with the boss last night," he said. "She's quite a lady. Never come across anyone like her before. I like a woman to wear French scent and make-up. She is so feminine."

"Yes, we all like Agatha, and are very protective of her," said Toni. "She has made mistakes with some awful men in the past, and so we all try to make sure she is never hurt again."

"I wouldn't call Charles awful."

"No, he isn't. And I think Agatha might have a chance; that is, if she didn't keep falling for unsuitable men."

"You're driving over the limit," said Jake.

"Sorry." Toni realised that she had become angry. Jake was making her feel inadequate. He was posh, ex-public school, and very handsome. Toni was used to men being immediately attracted to her. But here was this Adonis babbling on about Agatha, of all people. Was it because he thought she, Toni, was common? Her sense of humour came to her rescue, and she told herself that she was in danger of being jealous of Agatha. What a hoot!

"Do you have a girlfriend?" Toni found herself asking.

"Not at present. Hard to find the right girl."

I happen to be right here, thought Toni, getting cross again, or haven't you even noticed?

"Maybe if I had been living, like, you know, in the olden days, the Edwardians and all that lot. It would have been okay for me to go to Paris and get my rocks off with an experienced courtesan."

"You can pay for a tart just as easily in London today."

"Not the same," said Jake. "You see, those courtesans learned all about how to behave outside the bedroom as well as in it, you know, amuse and charm and discuss politics and books and all that. I get easily bored. Now Agatha isn't boring."

"I hope you are not thinking about having an affair with Agatha!" said Toni. She swung the car into a lay-by and stopped, swinging round to face him.

"Why not?" demanded Jake. "She's single."

"Look," said Toni, "for you it might just be getting your rocks off as you so elegantly put it, but Agatha might fall in love with you, and love is a responsibility."

"This is too serious," said Jake. "Don't worry. I'm too keen on this job to want to do anything to screw it up. Okay?"

"Yeah. Fine." Toni drove on. "We'll go to the hall first," she said. "To give you a rundown, Damian is feminine and weird. They're all weird. Daughter Andrea is the only one who really mourned Bellington. The wife is recovering from drink and drugs. Another oddball."

They checked in at the lodge and then moved on up the drive. "We've got a place in the country like this," said Jake. "Pa likes playing the squire."

"Is your mother dead?"

"Yes. She was a do-gooder. Women's Institute, Save the Church Tower, all that sort of thing. Sat on a lot of committees. Never did see much of her. Nurse, governess, then off to prep school. By the time she'd died of cancer, my mother seemed like some do-gooding stranger."

"Didn't that damage you emotionally?" asked Toni, coming to a halt outside the mansion.

"Not really. Don't know. Hadn't time to think with Pa shoving me into one job or another. Should have stood up to him before this. Poor old sod. He must be feeling lousy. So let's go and let me have a look at the zoo."

Damian greeted them with delight. "This is a treat. I do so like beautiful people. Read about you in the newspapers. Diamonds in the furniture. Wish there was some in mine. Oh, Andrea. What do you want?"

"I want to say hullo to the guests," said Andrea, gazing at Jake. "Is that a problem?"

"Never bothered before. Oh, sit down. How can I help?"

Jake, who had been reading up on the case, said, "The housekeeper, the old one, that is, she said Lady Bellington was down in the cellar with a syringe."

"Which turned out to be a lie," said Damian, "as you were already told."

"Would you like to see the cellars?" asked Andrea.

"That'd be great." Jake got to his feet. "Coming, Toni?"

"No need for both of you," said Andrea.

When they had gone, Damian grinned. "She'll eat him alive. Oh, Mother, what is it?"

"I was looking out of the morning room windows and saw the most delicious young man arriving. A friend of yours?" asked Lady Bellington.

"No, another detective. Andrea has dragged him off to the cellar from which he may never emerge."

"I'd better rescue the poor lad."

"Just you and me," said Damian with a grin.

"This is still a murder enquiry," said Toni. "And yet, you seem to treat the whole thing as a joke."

"If I didn't," said Damian, "I'd be as bonkers as the rest of the family."

The sun flickered through the ivy leaves half-covering the window and sent harlequin patterns flickering over Damian's face.

"That ivy," said Toni. "Don't you ever want to get it cut? It makes all the rooms so dark."

"I'm sure the factor will get around to it one day. Will you marry me?"

"What?"

"I'm asking you to marry me. Think about it. No more nasty murder cases."

"You don't even know me!"

"Don't have to. You're young, pretty, and would produce lovely babies."

"Let's get down to business," said Toni sharply. "If Mrs. Bull was talking rubbish about Lady Bellington being down in the cellar with a syringe, why should she end up down the well?"

"Because she probably had some real nasty gossip about someone else. Ah, it must be them tharr wicked aristos at the hall, thinks you. Wrong. That village is full of vice. Go away and turn over a few stones. Mother has a cast-iron alibi. She was in rehab, or the home for the bewildered, or whatever you call these places."

Toni sat outside in her car, wondering whether to go back in to rescue Jake, when he appeared. "You know," said Jake, sinking into the passenger seat, "they are all so mad that you begin to think you're the one who's odd."

"So what happened in the cellar?"

"Andrea groped my bum. Mother arrived, told her to lay off, told me to get on with whatever I was supposed to be doing, and stood there with her arms folded watching me while Andrea slouched off. There was really nothing I could do but beat a retreat."

"Oh, well, let's see if we have any more luck with this Humphrey Sanders at Pear Tree Cottage than Agatha had. He's the one who was angriest about Bellington raising the rents."

"Odd sort of place," commented Jake as they drove into the village. "No shops, no pub. There is a church. Look! There's a funeral taking place. Never tell me old Ma Bull has turned up her toes."

"Too soon," said Toni. "She was alive earlier today. Let's go and have a look."

She parked the car by the village green, and both got out and walked towards the church where the coffin was just being borne out and into the graveyard. "I really must see this," said Toni. "I didn't think they buried them in these old graveyards anymore."

"Must be Low Church," said Jake.

"What's Low Church?"

"Church of England without the bells and smells. High Church was considered too popish."

"So why do you think it's Low Church?"

"Coloured coats. No fancy hats. No black mourning."

As they walked into the churchyard, a woman approached them. "Are you friends of the deceased?" she asked.

"No," said Toni quickly, having a sudden instinct that Jake was about to lie. "We're detectives."

"Oh, yes, poor Mrs. Bull. Still holding on?"

"Yes, indeed."

"It's just that these old churchyard services are so beautiful," said Toni. "But we are sorry to have intruded."

"But you must stay. It's a celebration, in a way. I am burying my mother. She was horrible. Do join us."

They were in time to hear the vicar intone as the coffin was lowered into the grave, "Goodbye to you, Mrs. Clutter. You had a long and busy life, and now you can rest with the angels."

"Whatever happened to 'Man that is born of woman?'" hissed Jake.

A stocky man in front of them turned round and glared Jake into silence.

"You will be sorely missed by everyone," intoned the vicar, "especially your daughter, Cassandra. Good-bye from all of us."

"Very disappointing," whispered Toni. "They do it much better on television."

The woman who had first approached them caught up with them as they were leaving the graveyard. "I am Cassandra Clutter," she said. "We are having some refreshments in the village hall. Do join us."

"We are sorry for your loss," said Jake.

"Then you must be the only two people in the whole wide world who are," she said. "That's the hall over there."

"Posh voice," said Toni as they watched her walk away. "Come down in the world? I didn't see any grand houses in this hamlet of a place."

"There is one," remarked Jake. "Behind those trees at the back of the place. You can just see the chimneys."

"Then why not have the wake there?"

"Maybe too many people. Lots of them heading for the hall, a lot that weren't even at the service."

They were met by a roar of voices as they walked in. "Do help yourself to cider, m'dears," said a small woman. "It do be the best cider this side o' Devon. Humphrey does us proud."

"Would that be Mr. Sanders?"

"Yes, that be he, over there by the gurt barrel."

"I don't know that we can interview him here," said Toni. "We'd better wait until later. Let's try old Mrs. Ryan up by the allotments."

"Toni!" pleaded Jake. "Those sausage rolls they're handing round look delicious, and I'm aching to try the famous cider."

"Oh, well, a tankard each and then we'll get off."

"Thank you, mummy. You get the sausage rolls and I'll get the cider."

When Jake returned with the cider, he found Toni clutching a paper plate with four large sausage rolls on it.

"Let's take this stuff outside," suggested Jake.

They sat on a wall outside the hall. Both agreed the cider was excellent.

"It's a creepy sort of place," said Jake, looking about.

"What's up with it?" asked Toni. It was a sunny autumn day. Ducks sailed placidly on the pond. A gusty wind swung the branches of a willow tree, and its leaves, like little golden disks, flew out into the air.

"I don't know. Just a feeling. I think maybe we should wait on until later and perhaps have a word with Miz Clutter. She was so direct about her awful mother, she might be refreshingly blunt about other people here."

Jake surveyed Toni out of the corner of his eye. She really was very beautiful and had a sort of fresh, untouched air about her. He wondered whether she was a virgin and then dismissed that idea. They didn't exist anymore, at least not when girls reached their late teens. Toni had given up wearing her long blond hair straight and had slightly curled it and tied it back with a jaunty tartan ribbon. She suddenly turned and looked full at him, and blue eyes met blue eyes in a long fascinated stare. A delicate flush rose to Toni's cheeks while Jake fought down a sudden surge of elation. I'm in love, he thought. I haven't felt like this since . . . well, what *was* her name? But surely it wasn't like this.

Toni gave herself a little shake and said briskly, "I don't think we should have any more cider. It's getting noisier and noisier in there, and it'll probably go on for some time. Let's go and see Mrs. Ryan and tackle Cassandra later on."

They got into Toni's car after putting their paper plates in a garbage pail and returning the tankards to the bar.

"Here it is," said Toni, stopping outside Mrs. Ryan's house. "And she certainly has a good view of the allotments."

But although they rang the bell and knocked, there was no reply. "Maybe, if she's an old lady, she's having a nap," said Jake.

"Or for all we know, she might be swigging cider at the wake. I don't think the Church of England calls them wakes."

"No, they mumble politely 'Refreshments at the George' or wherever. Usually it's only selected guests, but I suppose it's a free-for-all in a place as small as this. I say, have you got a fellow?"

"I don't like personal questions," said Toni.

"You're so gorgeous, you must have. Marry me."

Toni burst out laughing. "You are an idiot. Let me look up and see if there's anyone else on the list. Ah, there's a Mary Feathers, head of the allotments. Quite near. We'll try, and if she's out, we'd better look for her and Mrs. Ryan at the party or whatever it is. Agatha has written 'Old bitch' next to Mary's name."

Mary turned out to be at home. "Two beautiful detectives!" she exclaimed, after they had introduced themselves. "Do come in. Have you been to the hall? Most of the village will be there for old Mrs. Clutter's funeral." Toni noticed the admiring looks Jake was giving Mary and felt a pang of jealousy, but reminded herself severely that Simon had been enough trouble. Better keep it out of the workplace.

"We've been there," said Jake. "We actually came to try to see Mrs. Ryan, but she isn't at home."

"You'll be trying to find out who attacked poor Mrs. Bull," said Mary. "I don't know why I call her poor because she was a walking sort of poison pen letter. How she ferreted out so many secrets is a mystery to me."

"I wondered if it might have something to do with the allotments," said Toni. "Allotments do seem to bring out the worst in people."

"My dear, the Hatfields and McCoys have nothing on this lot when it comes to feuds. They are so jealous of their patches of land that if a thistle seed blows over from someone's plot, there are cries of blue murder."

"So why does someone so beautiful and calm as you head the committee?" asked Jake.

"How sweet you are, my love. It's because I was voted in by all of them. I never quarrel, see. Just listen. Would you like some tea or coffee? Or I have my own dandelion wine."

"How do you make that?" asked Jake.

"Quite simple. Dandelion petals, sugar, oranges, water and yeast. Wait there. You must have a glass."

When Mary had left the room, Jake lay back against the sofa cushions, his hands clasped behind his head and his long legs stretched out in front of him, and said dreamily, "I could listen to that clotted-cream voice of hers all day."

"I feel we're wasting time," said Toni sharply.

"If you want to talk to Cassandra, you'll have to wait a bit."

Mary came in carrying a decanter and glasses. "Bit chilly in here," she said. She bent over the fireplace and struck a match to a pile of kindling. When the fire was blazing, she threw on some logs. "Now," she said, pouring out three glasses, "that's the taste of summer."

"It's delicious," said Jake after an appreciative sip, and even Toni said with surprise, "You could market this."

"Too lazy. I don't do much once the autumn's here and there's not much to do on the allotments. Now, old Mrs. Clutter, she made Cassandra's life hell. Used her as a sort of cross between a maid and a companion. Big house, they do have. Called Admiral's Lodge, though none of them Clutters was ever in the navy. Yes, we thought old Ma Clutter would live forever."

"How did she die?" asked Toni.

"Fell down the stairs."

"Pushed?"

"Never say that, my chuck. Cassandra never had a bit o' courage."

Somehow, they found themselves accepting a second glass. The day darkened outside, and Mary lit an old-fashioned oil lamp on a table by the window. The fire crackled. A large black cat slouched in and curled up on the hearth.

Jake had a half smile on his face and his eyes were closing. I think she's hypnotising us, thought Toni. She stood up abruptly and said sharply, "Jake! We must go!"

"Oh, dear, must we?" Jake stood up. "Thanks for the wine, Mary."

"Call any time," she said.

The doorbell rang. They followed Mary as she went to answer it. Charles Fraith stood on the step. "What are you doing here?" demanded Toni.

"Minding my own business," said Charles. "Don't let me keep you."

"Doesn't Agatha trust us to do the job?" grumbled Toni.

"He's not detecting. He's on a date," said Jake. "Can't say I blame him."

So much for "Will you marry me," thought Toni. Men were a faithless lot.

"Let's try the Clutter woman," said Jake. "Isn't it amazing how people hang on to their odd names? Like being called Smellie. You would think they might change for the sake of the children."

When they approached the hall, they found only a few stragglers and were directed to the house behind the trees that Jake had spotted earlier. Two stone gate-posts flanked the entrance to a short drive bordered by laurels, rhododendrons and two large monkey puzzle trees. The house was a large grey stone building, built, Jake guessed, in the Edwardian reign. The only oddity was that above the upper windows on the front of the house were stone human faces: ugly, frightening, scowling horrors. Jake pointed to them. "Isn't that awful? Didn't the builders get enough money? Or, it could be, there's madness in the family."

"Well, the heiress seemed sane enough." Toni rang the bell, an enormous white china round clearly marked BELL in black letters and set on a disc of brass. A small round bad-tempered woman answered the door. "What?" she demanded.

Toni knew that if she said they were detectives, this woman would slam the door on them, so she said instead, "Miss Clutter wanted a word with us after the funeral."

"What about?"

Jake stepped forward, "Look," he said haughtily, "just do your job and run and get her. Stop standing there with your mouth open. Hop to it!"

"No need to get cheeky with me, young man," she said, but she retired into the darkness of the hall behind her, leaving the door open.

"You were awfully rude," said Toni.

"I know. She's a bully and the only thing bullies understand is other bullies."

Cassandra appeared and said, "Oh, the glamorous detectives. Do come in. Mrs. Terry! Tea, please, and some of those leftover cakes from the funeral."

"You should be resting, that's what," said Mrs. Terry. "Tea, indeed, and your poor ma not cold in her grave."

"On the contrary, as my mother died last week, I am sure she is very cold indeed. Tea!

"Awful woman," said Cassandra. She pushed open a door on the left. "Have a seat. I'll light the fire. Do you know there isn't any central heating? Mother wouldn't have it."

"You will be able to get it now," said Toni sympathetically.

"Wouldn't waste a penny on this place. I'm selling up and going to—oh, I don't know—the south of France or somewhere I can sit in the sun and eat croissants."

Cassandra had a long, mediaeval type of face with thick curved white lids over pale grey eyes. Toni guessed her to be in her late fifties. A rumbling outside and clattering of dishes heralded the arrival of tea. Mrs. Terry entered pushing a huge mahogany trolley laden with tea canisters, hot water, milk, sugar and cakes.

"Thank you. Go away," said Cassandra. "Now, Indian or China?"

"Indian," said Jake. "Me, too," said Toni quickly, because tea was stuff that came in bags, according to her experience.

"Would you, young Jake, light the fire? I would have asked that tiresome woman to do it, but she would moan on about how we never had fires lit until the middle of November."

While Jake went over to the fireplace, Toni watched, fascinated, as Cassandra measured out tea leaves into a silver pot and added hot water. Then she selected another canister and went through the ritual again, selecting a different silver pot. "I prefer China tea," she said to Toni.

"In your situation, lady of the manor," said Toni

cautiously, "we thought that might make you a good observer."

"Oh, say it," said Cassandra waspishly. "Old maid. Spinster of the parish."

"I simply got the idea that you were above normal intelligence," said Toni, who hadn't thought anything of the kind but was anxious to repair any damage.

"That was once the case," said Cassandra. "I won a scholarship to Oxford, but my father died and mother became a permanent invalid. I adored my father and was shattered by his death, and so I became a blasted companion."

She strained a cup of tea into an eggshell-thin cup. "Milk and sugar?"

"A little milk and one lump," said Toni.

"What about you, young man?"

"No milk and four lumps," said Jake, sitting back on his heels and admiring the blaze. He got to his feet and sat on a sofa next to Toni. Family portraits hung on the walls. The furniture was solid and Victorian, apart from a handsome grand piano.

"Are these your ancestors?" asked Toni.

"Oh, no, they came with the house. Grandfather made his money up in Yorkshire. He owned several mills. When he died, Father sold the lot and invested the money. He didn't really do anything. He said he wanted to be really posh, and that is why he bought this house along with the ancestors and married Mother, who is related to the Earl of Ampweather, be it a mere twig on the family tree and to a family who showed absolutely no signs of ever wanting to know her. Of course, you want to know about this village and who could have attacked Mrs. Bull. The trouble is that she is such an awful woman, it could have been anyone. Now, Mrs. Ryan is your best bet."

"We tried there, but there was no reply," said Jake.

"I believe she sleeps in the afternoon. She is a very sharp observer of character. Do have some cake."

"May I use your bathroom?" asked Toni.

"Yes. It's at the top of the stairs."

Toni went up the oaken staircase. An unhappy house, she thought. The stairs were uncarpeted and polished to a high shine. As she neared the top, the dim light winking on something caught her eye. She bent down. A nail had been hammered into the side, and a knot of cord was still tied round out. Is that how her mother fell down the stairs, thought Toni. Do I report this? Do I cause this woman, who has escaped from her horrible parent, to suffer a police investigation?

But as she descended the stairs again, she knew she could not do it.

Cassandra was laughing at something Jake had just said as Toni entered the room. "It's getting late," said Toni. "We should go. Thank you so much for the tea."

"Call again, although I might not be here. I'm getting away as soon as I sell this place."

As Jake got into the car, Toni said, "I've left something. Back in a minute."

She sprinted back to the door and rang the bell. Cassandra answered it. Toni whispered urgently, "There is a nasty nail sticking out at the top of the stairs. Get pliers and get it out before Mrs. Terry sees it."

"Oh, thank you," said Cassandra calmly. "How odd I never noticed that before."

Chapter Eight

Although Toni and Jake were eventually able to speak to Mrs. Ryan, they could not elicit any more than Agatha had already had from her, although as far as Cassandra was concerned, she did confirm that old Mrs. Clutter had led her the hell of a life. Jake was puzzled because Toni looked worried and barely seemed to be listening.

Still, after Mrs. Ryan, they called on various villagers. It always seemed to be the same. Mrs. Bull was a nasty woman who liked finding out secrets about people. Was she a blackmailer? No, said everybody. She wasn't blackmailing *me*.

"Of course," said Jake, "not one of them is going to admit to having something in their own lives that was worth blackmailing them over. Toni! Toni, where are you?"

"Sorry, I'm a bit tired. Let's go home and type up the little we've got in the morning."

But after Toni dropped Jake off in Mircester, she began to think her guilty conscience would never let her sleep again, and so instead of going to her flat, she headed for Carsely.

Agatha answered the door, her face lit up like a ghoul with a green light at the end of an appendage sticking from her mouth. "Bloody e-cigarette," she said. "I'm beginning to think nothing will work. Come in. Have you anything exciting?"

"Yes," mumbled Toni, edging past her and making for the kitchen, where she crouched down on the floor and petted the cats. "You're not going to like it."

"Like a drink?"

"I'd love one, but I'm driving and I've already had cider and dandelion wine. Coffee would be great. What are you doing?" For Agatha was beginning to scrape the foil tops off little plastic tubs.

"I bought this lot by mistake. I've got that old-fashioned percolator, and these thingies are for that type of machine that George Clooney advertises. But I've got a cafetière. So if I scrape the gubbins into the cafetière, it makes a brilliant cup of coffee. Soon be with you. Just wait for the kettle to boil."

At last, the coffee was ready. Toni sat down at the table.

"Out with it," urged Agatha. "Nothing will shock me. I'm old enough to be your mo— . . . , elder sister."

"I think I've helped a murderer cover up a crime."

"Not Bellington! That's the only one earning me some money."

"No. Let me tell you about it." Agatha listened carefully to the story of Cassandra Clutter.

When Toni had finished, Agatha began to pace up and down. She was wearing a silk nightdress under a brightly coloured kimono, and the material made a swishing sound.

"Let me think," said Agatha. "Charles is here. I'll get him. I think he's fallen asleep in front of the television."

Another complication, thought Toni wretchedly.

But when Charles followed Agatha into the kitchen, he said, "What's all the fuss about, Agatha? If it's about me calling on Mary Feathers, then I'd like to point out that it's none of your business."

"It isn't that. What? Why?"

"Drop it, Aggie. I am allowed a personal life. What's this about Toni?"

Toni told her story again. "Oh, shite," said Charles. "Now you feel that Mrs. Bull might have found out about her pushing mum downstairs, and so Cassandra shoved her down the well."

"I didn't get as far as that," wailed Toni. "I only had this bad feeling I had helped her to cover up the murder of her mother. I was so sorry for her. I mean her mother seems to have made her life hell."

"Agatha and I will simply go down there tomorrow," said Charles soothingly, "and we'll tell her what's upset you, and then we'll both judge whether we think her guilty or not. But the police do investigate all sudden deaths. Don't worry. Let your elders and betters take care of you."

"You didn't tell Jake any of this?" demanded Agatha.

"No. Not a word."

"Good. Off you go. Try to get some sleep. Take over my work in the morning and allocate the jobs. Team Jake up with Phil."

The next morning, Agatha was unusually quiet on the road to Harby. Yet she would not admit to herself that she had come to regard Charles as her property. After all, he had gone off before and had actually become engaged. He had even been married. But for quite a time, he appeared to be fancy free. Autumn leaves danced and swirled in front of the car as if their twists and arabesques were mocking one middle-aged woman, reminding her that in the end, everything dies.

They arrived in Harby, and Agatha followed instructions to the house. Cassandra herself answered the door. After the introductions, Agatha said that they wished to speak to her about a really serious matter.

They were ushered into the drawing room. "I feel I am back at school and waiting outside the headmistress's study," said Cassandra. "You both look so grim."

Agatha gave Charles an appealing look.

So Charles told her of Toni's suspicions and how she was tormented by the fact that she had helped to cover up a murder.

"Oh, that!" exclaimed Cassandra. "Oh, that's nothing. That was Mrs. Terry. I told her right on the day mother died that she was sacked. Nasty, bullying woman. So she rigged up that nail and told people how I had put a cord across the stairs. It was after the police investigation. I told Mrs. Terry that her fingerprints were on that nail just to see her sweat."

"It's a wonder she didn't take it out herself," said Agatha, "or wipe the nail."

"That would be admitting she put it there. Oh, such good, good riddance to her and to sainted Mother."

"Did you never want to bump your mother off?" asked Charles curiously.

"Oh, so many times. But I am like Shostakovich."

"Is that a type of vodka?" asked Agatha.

"No. A Russian composer applied for membership of the Communist Party, even though he hated the lot of them. The evening before he was due to join, he broke down completely, calling himself a coward and a whore, saying he had been a coward all his life. That was me. Frightened of my own shadow. She broke me down, bit by bit, after Father died. I'm free at last. I'll travel. But I'll need to advertise for a companion because I don't even have the guts to go on my own."

"Perhaps a good psychiatrist . . ." began Charles.

"Don't believe in that mumbo jumbo."

"Oh, you should give it a try," said Agatha crossly, because she was still smarting at not knowing the name of that wretched composer.

"Worked for you, did it?" asked Cassandra.

"Unlike you, sweetie, I've never had need of one," snapped Agatha. "In fact . . ."

"In fact," interrupted Charles smoothly, "the other thing we wanted to ask you about was the murder of Bellington. Have you the slightest idea who might have done it?"

"He annoyed so many people. The village was furious because he was putting the rents up. I don't think his death has anything to do with Mrs. Bull. Such a nasty woman. Someone just broke. Mother liked dragging me up there when she was collecting for some charity or other. How she grovelled! In my opinion, the whole Bellington family is weird."

When they left Cassandra, Agatha felt depressed. "I don't think we're going to crack this case," she said gloomily. "Too many suspects, and now I've taken on useless Jake. As soon as I can find some work other than detecting for that young man, the better."

"That should teach you not to let your mind be seduced by good looks," said Charles.

"Oh, really? Then why are the other men in my life not at all handsome?"

"Bitch! Draw your claws in, Aggie."

And so they bickered amiably, not knowing Jake was going to make the first big break in the murders.

Jake had spent a pleasant enough day with Phil. But his work had mostly consisted of carrying Phil's camera bag while Phil snapped off shots of an adulteress.

Feeling restless at the end of the day, Jake took himself off to Carsely for a talk to Agatha, but finding her not at home, he went for a walk through the village instead.

He found himself up the hill and outside the ugly red brick cottage where Peta had lived. There was a pretty brown haired girl weeding in the garden.

Jake leaned over the hedge. "Do you usually weed by moonlight?" he asked.

She straightened up. "It's something to do. Do you want a coffee? I could do with one. I'm Peta's sister, Alison. You live in the village, yes?"

"No, I'm a detective."

Jake followed her inside. "Lot of cleaning?" he asked sympathetically.

"Fingerprint dust. Drawers turned out and nothing put back. I was surprised she left me the lot in her will. She never could stand me."

Jake followed her into the kitchen. Alison was late thirties, he judged. Older than he had first thought. She had a pleasant face and a round chubby figure, the bottom half crammed into jeans. She switched on the kettle. "It's instant, I'm afraid."

"Suits me," said Jake. "Can I do anything to help?"

"Maybe. I hate driving at night, and the lawyer gave me keys to a storage unit in Mircester. He should have given them to the police. Anyway, I'd like to have a look first."

"I'll drive you," said Jake. "Maybe we'll find something in there which will help us find out who murdered her."

To Jake's relief, George's Storage ran a twenty-four-hour service. They were shown to storage unit 204 and left in a dark alley lined with other storage units.

Alison unlocked the padlock, and Jake bent down and raised the door. He fumbled inside until he found an electric switch. Odd bits of furniture loomed up in the shadows cast by the weak light bulb overhead. Jake recognised some of it as being very good indeed. "What's that?" said Alison nervously, pointing to something wrapped in a blanket in the middle of the floor.

"Stand back," said Jake. "I'll look. It might be a body."

"Maybe we should call the police," said Alison nervously. "We could be mucking up a crime scene."

"They won't thank us if it turns out to be carpets." Jake whipped away the blanket, and both stared in amazement.

"What on earth is it?" whispered Alison.

"I know. It's a giant marrow. It's Harry Perry's giant marrow."

"Who's Harry Perry?"

"Some old boy from the allotments. I read it up in Agatha's notes. The villagers were complaining that someone was stealing their vegetables. Look, over in that corner. There's baskets of decomposing vegetables. Was your sister mad?"

"No, just spiteful," said Alison. "She always thought everyone in the whole wide world had it better than she had, and she would try to even the balance by stealing. Can't we just shut this place up and pretend we don't know? The thought of finding out which piece belongs to which person is too much."

"The police will do that," said Jake. "Look, this must be awful for you. Do you want to wait back in the car? I'd better phone the boss."

"No, I'll wait," said Alison. "We weren't close."

Agatha was getting ready for bed. Charles was staying the night. She had a sudden longing to invite him to join her, to hold her, to remind one middle-aged woman that there was still sexual life in her. "Don't go in for casual sex," nagged her conscience. "Why not?" she was just demanding when the phone rang. Agatha listened to Jake's excited description of his find. "Stay there!" she ordered. "I'll be with you as soon as possible."

Agatha blinked in the shadowy light of the storage unit. "She must have been some sort of kleptomaniac. Sorry, Alison."

Alison shrugged. "We weren't close. She punished people by taking something of theirs if they irritated her."

"I found this portrait," said Jake. He disappeared into the shadows and came back carrying an oil painting. It was a portrait of Nigel Farraday when he was younger.

"That's her ex," said Agatha. "Before I call the police, I want papers, a diary, something like that."

"Great detective finds secret diary in hidden drawer in antique desk," mocked Charles.

"Don't sneer. Let's all take a good look. No dead bodies here. So it's not a crime scene."

"It is, you know," said Charles.

They all stared at him. "What? Where?" demanded Agatha.

Charles pointed to the giant marrow. "You don't understand gardeners. To old Harry, that would be like pinching his child and leaving it to die."

"But if he didn't know where it was and didn't know she took it, there would be no reason to murder her."

"Unless she demanded money," said Alison in a sad little voice. "One of her favourite sayings was, 'I make people pay.' She liked power."

"So there might be letters or something somewhere here," said Agatha. "The police didn't find anything incriminating in her cottage, did they?"

Alison shook her head.

"If there's anything, it's probably in that briefcase by the door," said Jake.

They all swung round and followed his pointing finger. A black leather briefcase was placed behind a rocking chair next to the door.

"Shouldn't we leave it to the police?" said Alison.

"Just a peek," said Agatha.

Alison's normally pleasant features suddenly settled

into a mulish look. "No," she said firmly, "I don't want you poking around anymore. I will tell the police. She was, after all, my sister, and all that's left of our family."

"But, my dear girl," wailed Agatha, "in that briefcase there may be proof of who it was murdered Peta."

"I don't care," shouted Alison. "I want you all to leave. Now!"

"If that's the way you want it," said Jake. "I'll just switch off the light and help you to lock up." The storage unit was suddenly plunged into darkness.

"Put the light on now!" yelled Alison. "You're all leaving. I'm not. I'll phone the police now."

After some groping and fumbling in the dark, Jake found the light switch. When they got to the car park, Agatha said, "I'm phoning the police now before she destroys anything. I wonder what was in that case."

"Some sort of book," said Jake, producing it from under his jumper.

"Jake! If there is anything in there that leads us to the murderer, we can't use it. We should have left it for the police."

"Phil left me a camera to practice photographing documents," said Jake eagerly. "I'll sit in my car and bash off as many pics as I can, and then I'll sneak it back."

"Oh, go on," said Agatha. "But be quick. And here's a pair of gloves. Put them on."

Agatha fretted and tried not to chew her nails as Jake, in his car with the overhead light on, was busy clicking away. Then she heard the wail of a siren.

"That's it!" she shouted to Jake. "Get that book back."

Jake sprinted along to the storage unit. "Police on the way," he called. Alison was ferreting around in the shadowy depths of the unit.

Jake looked around and then threw the ledger over into a corner. It fell with a clatter. "What was that?" called Alison.

"Tripped on something on the floor," said Jake cheerfully. "I'll hang around and give you a lift home."

"No, I think I'll ask the police to take me back. I don't like the idea of private detectives snooping around. Something nasty and seedy about it."

When the police arrived, Jake made a brief statement. Then he followed Agatha and Charles to her cottage, where he put the pictures he had snapped into Agatha's computer.

"Is it a diary?" asked Agatha eagerly.

"No, it's nothing but a list of MPs expenses. Probably Farraday."

"Yes, he was involved in the expenses scandal," said Charles. "Look at the date. Years old. Must be right back to when she was married to him. Nothing of use."

Jake looked guilty. "There was a letter came with it.

Loose. Not part of the ledger. Maybe I shouldn't have taken it." He pulled a piece of paper out of his pocket.

"Oh, let's see it," said Agatha wearily. "Probably a grocery list."

"It's a bit of a letter," said Charles. He read aloud: "Peter's boy, Wayne, he saw you take my marrow, you bitch, and I am coming for you. Get it back here, or it will be the worst for you. I done been to the police, but they don't do nothing so I am taking the law into my own hands."

"Must be Harry Perry," said Agatha.

"Better show this to the police," said Charles.

"No," said Agatha. "I want to show Wilkes and Gerald that I am better than they are. I am going to get a confession out of Harry and take it to them."

"Great idea," cried Jake. He put his arms around her and kissed her on the cheek.

"Agatha, you are not even being paid to find out who killed Peta," snapped Charles. "It's vanity. You will put yourself at risk and get a spade in the back of your stupid neck. I'm going home."

"Ouch!" said Jake. "That was a bit nasty."

"He's not usually like that," said Agatha. "So let's go and wake the old boy up. I'll take a tape recorder."

As Agatha drove to the council estate at the edge of the village where Harry lived, she fretted about Charles.

She had felt somehow bereft when he had left in such an angry mood. She began to wish she had decided to leave any confrontation with Harry until the morning, but Jake was all excited, his handsome face alight, his blue eyes gleaming.

"Is he married?" asked Jake.

"I don't think so. I think there's something about his wife being dead in one of the notes on the case."

"Here we are," said Agatha. "The lights are on downstairs, and I can hear the television. What's the time? One in the morning. Bit late to go calling."

"No, we must do this," cried Jake. "You don't want the police to get there first."

"But we don't know he murdered her," fretted Agatha.

"Want the police to find out tomorrow?"

"No. Okay. Let's go."

Harry Perry answered the door. He was fully dressed but with three days' worth of unshaven beard, and he smelled strongly of spirits.

"We've found your marrow," said Agatha.

Harry looked at her in a dazed way. "You've found my Bertha?"

"Bertha?"

"Thas what I done call 'er. Bertha the Beautiful. I must go to her."

"The police have your marrow. May we come in?"

"Yes, come along. Oh, Bertha. Best ever."

They followed him into a neat, bright little parlour. Harry switched off the television.

Agatha switched on a powerful little tape recorder.

She was about to begin a slow interrogation when Jake said cheerfully, "Must have driven you mad, her pinching that marrow. Did you bash her on the head?"

"She jeered at me. She said she was going to give my Bertha to be cut up in a Chink restaurant. Her was standing there, laughing. 'Twas late at the allotments, and we was the only ones there. I took my spade and hit her on the head I was that angry. Didn't mean to kill her, but she was dead so I buried her."

Agatha said quietly. "The police will be coming for you, Harry."

He heaved a great sigh. "Well, now, it'll be a relief. I've always been a God-fearing man and never done no wrong to nobody. But, oh, what she done to Bertha was cruel."

"Bertha is in a storage unit," said Agatha. "Your marrow was not cut up. Would you like to come with us now? I think the police will still be at the storage unit, and you can see your marrow."

At the storage unit, Wilkes swung round in a fury as Harry rushed in and knelt down beside his marrow.

"What the hell are you doing here with that man?" shouted Wilkes.

"He wants to say goodbye to his marrow before he tells you how he murdered Peta Currie. I have his confession on tape," said Agatha. She felt it should be her moment of glory, but somehow Charles's angry face kept rising up in her mind.

It was a long night of interviews. At last, Jake and Agatha were free to leave. At Agatha's cottage, Jake said, "Mind if I stay? I'm exhausted."

"Charles has gone, so you can have the spare room."

Agatha petted her cats and went wearily up to bed as an angry red dawn was shining in the windows. She showered and climbed into bed—and found Jake already there.

"Lost your way?" demanded Agatha.

He gathered her in his arms and began to kiss her with single-minded intensity, and Agatha went down under him in a red sea of passion.

Toni said to Simon as they met in the office in the morning, "I got a text from Agatha. It seems she and Jake discovered Harry Perry to be the murderer of Peta. I wonder if she'll come in today."

"Probably our young friend has got his leg over by now."

"You have to be joking. She's old enough to be his mother."

"Yes, but he fancies her rotten. Saw it coming a mile off."

"I won't believe it," said Toni.

Agatha awoke the next morning with an anxious feeling that she had done something she really shouldn't have done. Memory came flooding back. Jake! There was no one in the bed next to her.

How could she have been so stupid? Oh God. Had Charles seen it coming? Agatha crawled out of bed and showered and dressed before going downstairs. Doris Simpson handed her a cup of coffee. "That young fellow said he would see you in the office."

"Yes, thanks," said Agatha. "Forgot something."

She sprinted up the stairs to her bedroom and stripped the sheets off the bed, ran back downstairs and stuffed them in the washing machine.

"I would have done that," said Doris.

"It's all right," said Agatha, switching on the washing machine.

"You forgot the soap powder," said Doris.

"Sod the soap powder," yelled Agatha. Immediately she followed it up with, "I'm sorry, Doris. Have just made a big mistake."

"Sit down, Agatha, love," said Doris. "He's a gorgeous-looking young man."

"It's not that," wailed Agatha. "He's on my staff. I can't bear the thought of having an affair with someone that people will mistake for my son. I can't bear the thought of all the maintenance and fear of wrinkles."

"Well, you have a talk to him. But he must have really wanted you. I mean a chap like that could get any girl he wanted."

The doorbell rang. "I'll get it," said Doris. She came back after a few moments. "It's the press."

Agatha sighed and got to her feet. "I'd better give them a statement. I've an agency to run, and it pays to advertise."

There was a great deal of press interest. A murder in a village was not great news. A murder over a giant marrow called Bertha, on the other hand, warranted the front page.

Agatha forced herself to mention Jake, but she was dreading seeing him again.

All the way into the office, she rehearsed speeches. But it was with a feeling of relief that she found the office empty apart from Mrs. Freedman, the secretary.

"All out of jobs?" she asked.

"Yes. Simon's looking for a lost teenager, Phil and Patrick both have divorce cases and Toni's taken young Jake off on a supermarket theft. Pleased as anything today is Jake. Thinks he fancies Toni. They make a handsome couple. I look at them and wish I were young again. Don't you feel that, Agatha?"

"No, I feel like work," said Agatha. "Tell everyone I've

gone back to Harby. Now that Peta's murder is out of the way, I can concentrate of what we're being paid for."

It was a sunny day. The countryside had turned into a sort of jewel box as the autumn leaves blazed in ruby, gold, silver and purple beside the road. But blind to all the beauty was Agatha Raisin. It wasn't the inner child she suffered from, she thought gloomily. It was that nagging inner governess. "How could you have been so stupid as to go to bed with that young man? Grow up. Act your age." She felt as if she had overindulged in chocolate or booze. She hoped Charles never found out. Then she gave herself a mental shake. Charles was a friend, that was all. But she seemed to see his accusing face in her inner mind. She wrenched her mind away from Jake. What had happened to Gerald Devere? She hadn't seen him around. The case should now be less complicated with Peta's murder being solved, but it could still have something to do with one of the allotment holders, furious that Bellington had meant to build houses on their land. That business with the diamonds in the furniture had nothing to do with Bellington. But it had landed her with Jake. Agatha winced.

As she turned into the drive at Harby Hall and waved to the lodge keeper, she realised that she did not have any reason to call. She parked in front of the main entrance, switched off the engine and rested her hands on the wheel. Agatha had not seen her friend, Mrs. Bloxby, for some time. She suddenly hoped that Mrs. Bloxby had got over her infatuation for Gerald. And thinking of infatuation, she thought grimly, I'd better let young Jake down gently.

Jake and Toni had enjoyed a successful morning at a large supermarket. They had been blaming loss of profits on shoplifters, but Toni and Jake, while pretending to be shelf stackers, had found that five members of the staff were blatantly stealing goods and using one of the supermarket's vans to cart the stuff away. Most of the stolen stuff was electrical: microwaves, vacuums, television sets and so on. Toni and Jake had filmed the thieves, Jake being amazed that the thieving was so blatant. The management called the police, the culprits were arrested and Toni and Jake left with praise ringing in their ears.

"I think this calls for a drink," said Jake.

Toni smiled. "Just this once."

They went into the nearest pub. Toni ordered a vodka and tonic and Jake had a half of lager. "I love this detective business," said Jake happily, "and I love you, Toni."

"Don't be silly."

Jake looked dreamily at the blond beauty that was Toni. He had practically forgotten his night with Agatha. That was just one of those things.

"Why don't we go clubbing this evening?"

"Because I've got a date," said Toni.

"Who with? Simon?"

"Mind your own business."

Agatha got out of the car. All she could do was tell them about Peta's murderer, study faces, try to pick up vibes and push and prod until something gave way. Andrea answered the door, scowling horribly. "In my opinion, you're a waste of space," said Andrea by way of a greeting. She turned and hurried off. Agatha shrugged and began to walk along the passage. There was a mirror at the end of it showing her reflection. She had recently lost weight, and her figure in a dark blue cashmere trouser suit was trim. Sun shining in from a high window shone down on her glossy hair. "Not bad," she said. "Not bad at all."

"What's not bad?" drawled a light voice behind her, making her jump.

Agatha swung round. "Oh, Damian, I was just thinking that with Peta's murder solved, it should surely make things less complicated."

"Let's talk." He pushed open the door of one of the hall's many rooms. This one was full of old hunting boots, crops and a couple of saddles and a child's rocking horse. "I should really get the decorators in," said

Damian, "and throw out half the stuff. I don't hunt, so what's the point of keeping all this rubbish?"

"Get a good antique dealer in to evaluate things before you throw anything away," said Agatha. "That rocking horse is surely worth a lot."

"Good advice. Find a seat. Talking of money, are you getting anywhere or am I wasting my poundses on the desert air?"

"No, I'm getting a good idea of what happened," said Agatha. "I don't want to tell you right now because I may be wrong, and you might unwittingly alert the guilty person."

"Do you want me to prepare the library?"

"What?"

"Well, you know. You call us all together and lean on the mantle and go through us, accusing us one after the other until you point and say, 'But it was YOU!'"

Agatha gave a reluctant laugh. "I would like to ask you about Mary Feathers. Allotments seem to bring out the beast in people."

"Our village siren. I think she's a lesbian."

"Meaning you tried and couldn't get anywhere."

"No. From time to time, Mary has the odd waif living with her. Sometimes they are seen hand in hand, which offends the delicate sensibilities of the villagers."

"I might have a word with her," said Agatha.

"You do that and hurry up. I am not a bottomless pit of money."

As Agatha stood outside Mary's cottage, she wondered if Charles had called on the woman for a date. What if Charles ever found out she had been to bed with Jake? Agatha shrugged. It was none of his business. He had made no commitment to her. On the rare occasions he had visited her bed, he had not uttered one word of love. Her eyes suddenly filled with tears, and she blinked them away to find the door had quietly opened and Mary was surveying her.

"You could do with a strong cup of tea," said Mary. "Come in and sit by the fire."

Weakly, Agatha followed her in. A bright fire was burning on the hearth, and the room smelled of apples and cinnamon. "Sit down, and I'll fetch tea."

Agatha began to think up excuses, maybe saying something like, "I had some grit in my eye," but decided just to ignore the whole thing.

Mary came back and placed a side table by Agatha's chair. On it she placed a cup of tea. "Milk? Sugar?"

"Straight up," said Agatha with a weak smile.

Mary settled herself in an armchair opposite. "You'll be wanting to know if I had any gossip or if I've heard anything. Just speculation, my dear. Now, Mrs. Bull is such an evil gossip, it's a wonder no one's attacked her before this. She put it about that I was seducing innocent young girls. I belong to the Big Sisters Club. We sort of adopt some waif or stray and take them out from time to time. Did I threaten the old bat? Sure I did. Said unless she got her gossip right, I'd hex her. Lot of them think I'm a witch. Feeling better?"

"Yes," said Agatha. "You surprise me. You were not all that friendly before."

"Sorry. I get malicious sometimes."

"Why?"

She stretched and yawned. "Boredom, mostly. So I mix things up. I thought if I could get that Charles of yours interested, it would annoy you."

"Why?" asked Agatha.

"Jealousy, my love. I'm jealous of women with careers."

"So did it work?" asked Agatha. "Charles, I mean."

"He only came back in with that story about having left his wallet to get at you. Don't you pay him enough attention?"

"He's not all that interested in me," said Agatha, "and he'll be even less interested if he finds out what I've done."

"And what's that? Can't be nothing too bad."

Lulled by the warmth of the fire and the caressing voice opposite, Agatha told Mary about her night with Jake.

There was a sudden change of atmosphere in the room, as if the temperature had suddenly dropped. Agatha gave herself a mental shake and rose to her feet. "I'm wasting detecting time, burdening you with my troubles," she said. "Thank you for the tea. If you hear anything, let me know."

When she had left, Mary went to her desk and searched through a little pile of cards until she found one marked Charles Fraith. It had his e-mail address on it. Mary switched on her computer and began to type.

Agatha would have been furious if she had known how little her night with Jake had troubled him. Jake was typical of a lot of young men in thinking that middle-aged women should be grateful for a roll in the hay and not expect anything more than a one-night stand. His attention was firmly fixed on Toni. That was love.

But late that afternoon, Charles walked into the office. "Agatha around?" he asked.

"Due back later," said Toni. "We're just finishing up here."

"Like to go for a drink, Toni?" asked Jake while Simon glared.

"Shouldn't you wait for Agatha, Jake?" asked Charles in a deceptively quiet voice.

"Don't need to. I've typed out my report. She'll be pleased. Had a successful day."

"And a successful time last night in her bed, I gather," said Charles.

Toni looked shocked, and Jake turned deep red. "We were both a bit drunk and . . . and . . ."

"Tell her I'll call her later," said Charles.

After he had left, Toni said, "Agatha is not as tough as she looks. I think you should buy her flowers or something."

"But, Toni. It didn't mean anything," wailed Jake.

"Come on, Simon," said Toni. "Let's go to the pub."

Agatha arrived back at the office at eight o'clock in the evening. She saw to her surprise that the lights were still on and even more surprised to find Jake sitting at his desk with his head in his hands.

She stopped on the threshold. Jake was really very handsome.

"Waiting for me?" she asked.

"Yes. I've made a mess of everything, and Toni won't look at me," said Jake bitterly. "Charles is a bastard."

Agatha sat down slowly. She had sworn off cigarettes that day, but she found herself scrabbling in her handbag for a pack of Bensons and a lighter. She lit a cigarette and studied the trail of smoke rising up to the fluorescent light and said quietly, "What has it to do with Charles?"

"You shouldn't have told him we spent the night together!"

"I didn't! I've been down at that poxy village getting absolutely nowhere. So who told him?"

"He just seemed to know. Oh, what a bloody mess."

And that's a verdict on a night of lovemaking, thought Agatha wearily. What a bloody mess, indeed.

Agatha surveyed Jake. "Think young man! I am not made of iron. I am not your nanny or anyone's mother figure. And yet you sit there worried about having ruined your chances with Toni?"

"It's different," said Jake. "You're an experienced woman."

"Oh, you're down in the hole already so stop digging. Any messages?"

"One from *Gloucester BBC*. They're doing a women-in-men's-jobs week and they've been let down by a woman bricklayer and wondered if you could hop along to the studio at eleven o'clock tomorrow morning."

"Phone them in the morning and say I can't make it. No, phone them now. They're a decent bunch, but I don't feel up to it."

Jake reached for the phone. "Leave it!" said Agatha suddenly. "I've an idea, I'll go after all. Now, I am off to bed . . . alone, now and forever. Try for a bit of empathy and humanity. It helps detecting."

As she turned into Lilac Lane and parked in front of her cottage, Agatha looked nervously around for Charles's car. Why should I care? she chided herself. But she set off again and drove to the vicarage.

"Is it too late for a chat?" she asked as Mrs. Bloxby answered the door.

"No, Alf's over at Ancombe and won't be back until late. Come in."

In the soft lights of the vicarage drawing room, Agatha studied her friend. The hair was still dyed a soft brown, but she was wearing one of her old droopy skirts and a shirt blouse.

Agatha sank into the old sofa and laid her head against the feather cushions. She dreamily watched the flames on the wood fire on the hearth and felt at peace.

"I've made a bit of a mess of things," said Agatha.

"Sherry?"

"Yes, please."

Agatha waited until a glass of sherry was placed in her hand. "It all seemed so awful, so disgraceful, but now I am here, it doesn't seem all that important. You see, I went to bed with young Jake last night. Both of us were drunk and it just happened. But Jake is in love with Toni and looked on me as part of getting drunk and somehow Charles found out. I confronted Jake in the office, and he said he'd lost his chance of getting anywhere with Toni. So here I am. Some ghastly Mrs. Robinson."

"A lot of women would envy you. A young man like Jake could have his pick."

"But what on earth has it got to do with Charles? Honestly, Sarah, I don't understand that man."

"You called me Sarah!"

"About time. It was fun when the Ladies Society was operational. I always wanted to be a lady. So Mrs. This and Mrs. That seemed OK."

"One gets possessive of one's friends," said Mrs. Bloxby. "I mean, you have no interest in your ex-husband, but you get quite jealous if he is squiring someone else."

"Why is it that men can hop in and out of bed without any sort of flashes of guilty conscience, and women are left to feel dirty?"

"It is called femininity," said the vicar's wife.

"Oh, all that womanly stuff. That went out with the birth control pill," said Agatha. "Now, it's come to bed or pay for your own dinner."

"Perhaps we are not *earthy* enough," said Mrs. Bloxby. "A lot of the village women would look on a night with Jake as a gratifying bit of slap and tickle. They wouldn't be sitting round under clouds of black guilt. Maybe it is one of the penalties one has to pay for being a lady."

Agatha grinned. "A lady. Me! I like that."

But when she reached home, she found Jake on her doorstep. He slipped an arm around her waist. "Let's go inside," he whispered.

Agatha backed off and glared at him in the security light above the door. "Sod off, you randy pillock," she yelled. "In future, remember I'm your boss and a lady and not some bedpan. Scram!"

Jake gave her one horrified look and sped to his car.

"And that felt good," Agatha told her cats as she sat on the kitchen floor and petted them. "I am giving up sex and cigarettes. From now on."

It was an odd autumn, thought Agatha as she headed to Gloucester the following morning. The leaves were turning, but the colours were more crayon than paint, as if some child were deciding, "I'll colour this one yellow, and this one orange and again yellow and maybe red."

The car park at BBC Gloucester was the usual nightmare of trying to find a space. Agatha managed to ease her car in by damaging the wing mirror on an old Ford. She went round to the reception area to report the damage to the wing mirror and leave details of her insurance for the owner. "It's a very old car," said the receptionist. "Wait a minute." She disappeared and came back a few minutes later. "All done. I just clicked it back into place."

There is always something kindly and cosy about local

BBC radio stations, reflected Agatha. They do so much for the local communities. Certainly, they were worth thinking of when yet another pseudo-Scandinavian crime thriller clunked onto the screen and made everyone wonder if the licence fee gave value for money. And why did TV detectives have to be riddled with mental problems and angst? Thank God for Colombo. No private life. Saved from even seeing Mrs. Colombo.

"Mrs. Raisin? Come this way." Agatha walked through to the studio to be interviewed by Claire Carter.

Nancy Sinatra was belting out, "These Boots Are Made for Walkin'," as Agatha took a seat at a microphone facing Claire, who switched off the sound and said, "I will be asking you if being a woman in a traditional man's job a drawback or an advantage. You've been on before, Agatha, so you'll know what to do."

Claire was a deft and experienced interviewer, one of those rare birds who can get people to relax and bring out the best in them. Agatha explained that woman's intuition was a valuable tool as she did not have the benefit of autopsy reports, DNA or other forensic reports. "So it's observation and guesswork," said Agatha. Claire broke off to give a travel report and play another record. "I'd like to ask your permission to appeal to the public for help in the murder of Lord Bellington."

"Go for it," urged Claire.

So when Claire came back on again, she said, "Agatha is going to ask you, the folk out there, for your help. Go ahead, Agatha."

Agatha succinctly outlined what she knew about the murder of Lord Bellington and then said, "Someone out there knows something. I feel it. One of you knows who this murderer is, and unless you step forward, I fear this person may murder again. He or she is ruthless. Poor Mrs. Bull was thrown down the well and nearly died. If you have any information, however slight, phone this number." Agatha gave out her three office numbers and the e-mail address. "Think hard," urged Agatha. "If there is another murder, and you knew something and did nothing to stop it, then you are as guilty as if you committed the murder yourself!"

As she moved out of the car park, Agatha began to fret. I hope that gets to someone, thought Agatha. Oh, I do not want to go to the office and run into Jake and all his rampaging hormones. Why am I so squeamish? A lot of women my age would be thrilled to bits. Look at all those sad sacks who read *Fifty Shades of Grey*? Maybe I'm old-fashioned, out of date. But I do crave romance. What woman doesn't? What are all the poems about, the love songs, the yearning? Surely I'm not alone?

She became aware her phone was ringing. She fiddled her hands-free apparatus and asked, "Yes?"

"It's Nigel Farraday. I need your help. I may have something for you."

"Lost our wallet again? I am rather busy."

"No! Listen. It's important. Don't come here. Do you know the Green Man at Ossbury?"

"No, but I'll find it. I'm in Gloucester. Is Ossbury near you?"

"You go through Chipping Norton and go on as if heading to Oxford. Turn off at the Glympton Road, and a few hundred yards along on the left is the pub."

"Okay. Give me about an hour to get there," said Agatha and rang off. She then rang Toni and told her where she was going.

The day was turning dark, and rain began to smear the windscreen. The wind rose, and swirls of coloured leaves danced about her car. Agatha felt suddenly hungry. Surely it wouldn't matter if she were a few moments late. She pulled into a garage with a Tesco Express store and bought an egg sandwich and two cans of Red Bull. She felt guiltily that she should have bought a healthy fruit drink instead. "My life these days," said Agatha to her car windscreen as she sat in the garage car park, "seems to be one long guilt trip so the hell with it." She popped open a can and drank the contents. When she finished her egg sandwich, she checked her face. Egg sandwiches, she knew, can be tricky beasts, depositing little clumps of egg unnoticed beside the mouth. Was that a wrinkle? "I'm fifty-three, that's all," she told the mirror. "That's the new forty."

A man knocked at her window, and Agatha lowered it. "Sorry to trouble you, but my wife and I are having an argument. She says you are talking to yourself. I said you were on a hands-free phone. Which is it?"

Agatha looked at him in amazement. "It's cold and raining," she said. "Get a life."

She shut the window and drove off.

Chapter Nine

J ake was feeling sulky. They treated him like a pariah at the morning briefing, although he brightened when he was told that he was to accompany Toni. Toni had told him firmly that if Charles called again, Jake was to say he had never bedded Agatha and that they had all been joking at Charles's expense. He was just about to leave with Toni where he got a peremptory call from the police to say he had to present himself at New Scotland Yard at two in the afternoon to be interviewed regarding the murder of Toby Cross. He caught the looks of relief as he made his excuses and left the office. He paused on the stairs and heard Simon saying loudly, "I wish the police would find out he did murder Toby and get the randy bastard out of our lives."

You'd think I'd screwed Miss Marple, thought Jake furiously, instead of a sexy woman who is . . . what? Late forties? Somehow he must put things right. It wasn't all about Toni. He loved the job and felt he could be good at it. He brightened. Maybe if he played the eager, willing-to-help role with the police, they might give him some titbits about the Bellington case.

Nigel Farraday waited for Agatha and wondered what story to give her. He wanted revenge because her report had ended in arrest and stopped from driving for a month. "Oh, get over it," his wife had said. "I'm off to help at the sale of work in Harby. Dead bore but I've got stuff I want rid of, and those old village tarts will buy anything."

"Help me. What shall I tell her to get her running in the wrong direction? And I want her to drink over the limit. *Then* I'll report her and see how she likes that. My pet PC Plod at Mircester said a pal of his saw Agatha in the phone box when I drove off that night."

"They'll all wonder why you didn't open the fête

this year as Damian refused and they're stuck with Lady Bellington and they can't stand her."

"Oh, tell them I know who murdered Bellington, and I'm meeting her in a secret rendezvous at the Green Man on the Glympton Road to spill the beans. May as well stir up the peasantry. Maybe someone will oblige me by doing her in."

"You do waste your time on petty revenge," snapped his wife. "Oh, go on. Men! Schoolboys all of them."

Agatha could not find any pub called the Green Man and began to wonder if Nigel was maliciously sending her off on a wild goose chase. At last, after knocking on doors, an old man told her it hadn't been called the Green Man for some years and was now the Hen and Basket.

Suddenly reluctant to join him now that she was parked outside the right pub, Agatha got slowly out of the car. A tall tree in the car park had one large branch scraping against another in the wind, and it gave out a ghostly creaky sound like the door of Count Dracula's castle being slowly opened.

She walked over to a sign that said LOUNGE BAR, walked down a short flight of steps and opened the door. It was an old-fashioned pub with a log fire at one end and high settles forming booths in front of tables. Agatha suddenly found herself thinking of Charles. She felt almost as if he were standing beside her. She shrugged off the feeling and went from table to table. There were only four men at one table and a couple, looking like elderly man and wife, at another.

She walked up to the bar. "I was to meet someone here, a Mr. Farraday. My name is Raisin. Has anyone been asking for me?"

"No, no one of that name."

"I'll have a gin and tonic."

"I'm sorry, our ice maker has broken down, but the tonic will be out the fridge."

"Okay."

Agatha took her drink over to a settle by the fire. Outside the wind grew stronger, and a flurry of beech nuts struck the glass, making her jump nervously. She looked at her watch. It had taken her just a little over an hour to drive from Gloucester. The settle was very old and very hard. Agatha thought it might have originally been a church pew where the Sunday sinners were not supposed to relax and get comfortable. As if reading her thoughts, the barman came over and handed her a cushion. "Forgot to give this to you. The regulars always know to ask for one. Ready for another?"

Agatha would have loved another, but she suddenly wondered if that was what it was all about. Maybe Nigel hoped to turn up by the time she had exceeded the limit and then report her. "I'll have a black coffee instead."

"Will you be wanting lunch? We've got lamb and leak pie, and it do go quick."

"Keep one for me," said Agatha, beginning to relax. She turned her mind to the problem of Jake. Charles didn't actually *know* anything. She would get hold of Jake and tell them it was all a joke and 'you should have seen your faces' type of thing. But it really isn't fair, she thought. If I'd been a fellow bedding down a young miss everyone would envy me. Man—a bit of a dog. Woman—dirty old bitch. Whatever happened to women's lib? One of those grand ideas, like the European Union, that kept unravelling. Where is this wretched man? She phoned Toni and told her where she was telling her the pub's name change. To her relief, Toni told her that they had all decided she had not passed the night with Jake and would inform Charles of that.

Charles was in Mircester when he heard Agatha's broadcast. He went up to the office. Toni told him that Agatha was waiting for Farraday at a pub in Glympton called the Hen and Basket. Then she said awkwardly, "I'm sorry. We shouldn't have let you go on thinking that Jake spent the night with Agatha. He didn't."

After studying her face, Charles said, "I'd better get

over to that pub. Goodness knows what she's stirred up. The Glympton road is only half an hour from here."

Nigel Farraday knew he was late. He had suffered from a punctured tyre and, not knowing how to change a tyre, had to wait for the Automobile Association to turn up. He phoned Agatha and told her to sit tight. Tight by now with any luck, he thought with a grin.

He found to his annoyance that the pub had changed its name. He had known the old landlord of the Green Man who, for a good tip, would have been happy to ply Agatha with very strong drinks. Like most people with drink problems, Nigel assumed Agatha was like he was himself, that once started, it was hard to stop. He pulled into the car park and got out. He saw a face he recognised and exclaimed, "What the devil are you doing here?"

"Get in your car. Got some news for you. It'll only take a minute."

Charles drove into the car park of the pub. He scowled at the large black Bentley. Farraday must just have arrived. He could see him in the front seat.

A great gust of wind sent spirals of coloured leaves whirling up. The tree with the odd branches groaned like a voice from the pit. Charles half-turned to go to the pub entrance when he suddenly looked back. Surely Farraday had not gone to sleep.

He went up to the Bentley and rapped on the driver's window. Nigel was lying back, his eyes closed. Impatiently, Charles jerked open the car door, and Nigel's lifeless body slowly fell out onto the ground.

The forces of law and order, remarked Charles later, were like the millstones of the gods, which, according to Euripides, ground slow and exceedingly small. And Agatha, who hated literary quotations with all the passion of the badly educated, told him to stop talking rubbish. They were sitting side by side in the waiting room at Mircester headquarters, having suffered long initial interrogations at Chipping Norton police station.

"I wish they would find out how he was killed," mourned Agatha. "The wife has been in there for ages."

"They hate giving us information," said Charles gloomily. "The press are out in the car park. No one told us not to talk to them. I wonder if one of them managed to get a word with the wife. Look, I'll nip out. You say I've gone for a pee."

Charles came back after ten minutes. "Haven't a clue," he said. "You'd better see if Patrick can find out something after the autopsy."

Agatha couldn't stand Charles's black mood.

"I didn't sleep with Jake," said Agatha. "You said I did!"

"If you didn't, you didn't. Nothing to do with me."

"If it's nothing to do with you, then why did you swan into my office and accuse me?"

"Well, it's like this, Aggie. We've always had something a bit other than friendship between us, haven't we?"

Agatha felt suddenly breathless. "Yes," she whispered.

He gave an awkward laugh. "You see, the mad thing is, I've been seeing this girl, and I am frightfully keen on her, and in some mad way, I felt disloyal to you. Isn't that crazy?"

"Totally mad," said Agatha. "Let's talk about something else."

"So you don't mind?"

"Why should I? Why now? You've had various romances over the years and so have I." But Agatha felt as if she had just descended in an overfast lift. She meant a roll in the hay to Jake, and an occasional bedfellow for Charles, and nothing to no one. Self-pity caught her by the throat. Agatha had an awful feeling she might cry and hailed the arrival of Bill Wong with relief.

"You can leave for now, but you will probably both be questioned further," said Bill. "Wilkes says you are not to speak to the press. I've to get you out the back door."

"Our cars are out front in the car park," protested Charles.

"Give me your car keys, and I will get a couple of officers to take the cars round the back."

Grumbling, they handed over their keys. Just as Bill left, Patrick walked in. "Meet me in the Jolly Farmer at the back of the square. Got some news."

Bill should have realised that the press would simply follow the cars round to the back, so Agatha held a press conference despite the fact that Wilkes was glaring down at her from an upstairs window.

In order to shake off the press once Agatha had finished speaking, they went back into headquarters, rushed out the other side and made their way through back lanes to the Jolly Farmer. Patrick was sitting staring down into a pint of beer. He could never look anything other than a copper, thought Agatha, even though he had been working now as a private detective for some time. From his open-pored lugubrious face to his black socks and highly polished black shoes, he screamed police.

When they were settled over drinks, Agatha asked eagerly, "What have you got?"

"What I've got is why he was killed," said Patrick. "He planned to go to the pub in Glympton, get you liquored up and have you reported and charged for drink driving."

"I always wonder why it is called drink driving and not drunk driving," said Agatha. "I mean, I'm drinking soda and lime and . . ."

"Oh, do shut up, Aggie," said Charles. "What did you find out, Patrick?"

"His missus was invited to open the sale of work at Harby. She didn't say he had gone off to Ossbury to try to get you arrested, Agatha. She tells everyone he's gone to tell you the name of the murderer. He told his wife it would stir up the peasantry. Amazing! The lower class people are, the more snobbish they get," said Patrick sanctimoniously.

"So the police idea that he had suffered from a heart attack is wrong," said Agatha. "Who was at the sale of work?"

"All the village of Harby and the lot of them from the hall."

Agatha stifled a yawn. "I'm tired. I need to get home and think."

When Agatha and Charles reached their respective cars, Charles turned and gave her a hug.

Agatha stood by her car and watched him drive off, wondering why she should feel so bereft. She had a sudden consuming desire to see this female who had so enchanted Charles. She decided to take the following day off and see if he could at catch a glimpse of her.

Agatha found Jake waiting for her. "Oh, for heaven's sakes, you randy bastard . . ." she was beginning when he interrupted. "It's not that. I've been in Scotland Yard for most of the day."

"The diamonds?"

"Yes."

"Come in," said Agatha, "but make it quick. I'm tired."

When Jake was seated at the kitchen table, he said, "It's all very hush-hush. The Malimbian Embassy produced a murderer but insisted he had been shipped home to Malimbia to face justice there."

"Sure the British police aren't going to allow that?"

"The Malimbians said that Toby was using their furniture to smuggle the diamonds to this criminal at the embassy."

"Still don't get it."

"They've discovered oil in Malimbia."

"I begin to get it. Maybe," said Agatha. "So why call you in?"

"Not flattering. We've all signed the Official Secrets Act, but they think because of my youth and the reputation my father has given me that I am some loose cannon, so I was threatened this way and that of all the dire things that would happen to me if I opened my mouth."

"Well, thanks for letting me know. I've had a horrid day." Agatha told him the latest news.

"Are you all right?" asked Jake.

Agatha shrugged, "I'll survive. But there is one important thing. I told Charles we didn't do anything, and everyone else thinks we didn't, so that episode is over."

"I'm an episode?"

"In my latest book," said Agatha. "Go home."

When he had gone, Agatha sat on the floor with her cats on her lap. "What excuse will I give for taking the day off?" she said, stroking their soft fur. "The trouble is, if I say I've got a cold, I'm bound to get one. Sod's Law. I'll just tell them I want a day off. No excuses."

By morning, Agatha began to feel that spying on Charles was grubby, but curiosity drove her on. The difficulty could be to spy on him without someone spotting her. It was easy to follow someone in town unobserved, but in the country, there were acres of nothingness where one could easily be seen.

From the gates of his estate, one road led east and the other west. Smoke was rising from the lodge chimney. Charles did not have a lodge keeper but had rented out the property, Agatha remembered, to a married couple. Agatha drove on, feeling exposed. She drove on out of the area and pulled off the road and phoned Charles. She was in luck in that he actually answered his mobile. Usually he let Gustav, his gentleman's gentleman, answer it.

"I'm doing some shopping in Stratford around lunchtime," said Agatha. "Fancy joining me for lunch?"

"Actually, I've got a date with Olivia, you know, the one I'm keen on. We'll be in the Golden Gander at one o'clock. Why don't you join us?"

"Yes, fine. Thanks," said Agatha bleakly. She could not remember Charles sounding so animated or happy before. What on earth are you playing at? her inner voice yelled at her. He's not yours. Never has been.

Agatha would not admit that somewhere in a little corner of her mind she had seen herself and Charles eventually settling down together.

Her phone rang. Charles again. "James is back," he said, "so I invited him as well. Olivia can meet my two oldest friends. See you."

I didn't even know James was back, thought Agatha. What happened to the days when I yearned and burned for him and now I don't feel a thing, not a twitching hormone in my whole body.

She looked at her watch. It was still only ten in the morning. Time to go into battle.

By the time Agatha reached the restaurant, her face had been made-up by an expert beautician, and her hair was washed and shining. She was wearing a scarlet ankle-length fun fur coat over a dark green cashmere trouser suit with high-heeled calf-length boots of black suede.

James and Charles were already seated. Both men rose. James kissed her on the cheek and said, "You are glowing, Agatha. Is the village gossip real? Have you been seduced by a young Adonis?"

"I wish," said Agatha. "Charles, where's the lovely Olivia?"

"Late as usual, I should think. Oh, here she is."

Both men rose to their feet. Charles held out a chair for Olivia, and she sat down facing Agatha. Olivia was startled. Somehow, from Charles's stories about Agatha, she had expected a hard-faced dumpy woman, not this glossy epitome of sophistication.

Olivia was twenty-eight. She had enjoyed coming out at the Season. It had cost her parents close to one hundred and twenty thousand pounds. Of course, it was no longer a marriage market. Jobs were fashionable. Charity extremely okay. She had worked as a secretary at a fashion magazine but had walked out the week before because the fashion editor had shouted at her. Olivia may not have looked on the London Season as a marriage market, but her old-fashioned parents, Jeremy and Beverley Huntington, certainly did, and were already grumbling about the lack of grandchildren. Charles was the answer to a prayer. Of course, he was in his forties, but his estates were pretty prosperous. The Huntingtons were extremely rich, having made their money in tea, which was alright, tea and beer both trades that had always been considered fashionable.

Jeremy Huntington's one regret was that his grandfather had not seen fit to grease Lloyd George's palm with money and get a title. But a married Olivia would be Lady Fraith, and that warmed his heart.

It was unfortunate that Olivia had a cold. Her nose was pink, and she was wearing a bulky Aran sweater over a pair of jeans and flat boots. Her hair was tinted blond but was worn straight, hanging down on either side of her face except when she suddenly swung a wing of it back, causing, at one point, James to duck. She had a high drawling voice where every word seemed to sound like "Yah." Not so long ago, Agatha would have felt intimidated, hoping that none of her original Birmingham-slum background was showing through the veneer, but she suddenly felt sad because she saw the attraction in Olivia, and it was, she was sure, quite simply money. She had forgotten that Charles was mercenary and also cared deeply about his home and estates. She often wondered why. His ugly Victorian mansion was hardly a national treasure.

Agatha had planned to compete with Olivia, to chatter, to brag, to dazzle. Instead, she recommended a good cold cure, suggested if Olivia wanted another job on a fashion magazine then that she, Agatha, knew a great woman on *Fabfash* who might like to employ her. Only Charles, his shrewd eyes moving from one to the other, guessed accurately that Agatha had sussed out his motives for courting Olivia and was actually sorry for the girl.

Her phone rang in the middle of the meal. James had been happily talking about his days in the army because Olivia's father had served in the Household Cavalry. Agatha excused herself and walked a little away from the table. It was Toni on the phone. "Mrs. Freedman is off ill. She's got shingles. Awful for her. Shall I get a temp?"

"Yes," said Agatha. "No. I might have someone. Call you back."

When she returned to the table, she said to Olivia, "My secretary is off with shingles."

"How too utterly ghastly," said Olivia. "My grand-mother had that, right down the side of her face."

"Are you feeling too awful?" asked Agatha. "Or could you help me out?"

"I say, Charles," exclaimed Olivia. "Isn't it exciting? I'd like to see the inside of a detective agency."

Agatha's ex-husband looked at her quizzically. Why was Agatha practically adopting this girl? There weren't any jealous vibes coming from Agatha.

After lunch, which, to the amazement of everyone except Olivia, Charles paid for, Agatha told Olivia to follow her to Mircester. Once in the car park, Agatha urged Olivia into her own car and produced a whole box of make-up and a magnified mirror, telling the girl she would feel better with a bit of foundation and lipstick.

Olivia followed Agatha into the office. The very first person she saw was Jake, sitting at his desk. Her mouth dropped a little open. Before Agatha could even introduce her, she said, "Hi! I'm Olivia, temporary secretary."

"You planned this all along," sneered the voice of Agatha's conscience.

"Leave me alone and just bugger off for once in your life," snapped Agatha, and then turned brick red as she realised she had spoken aloud.

"Sorry," she said, taking off her coat. "Thinking about something else. Patrick, anything yet on Farraday's death?"

"Not yet. But someone told me the pathologist had found a puncture mark on the arm."

"He wouldn't let just anyone get into the car beside him and stab him with a syringe full of something, would he? Must be someone he knew. Toni, check up the wife's background. Jake, could you settle Olivia in at Mrs. Freedman's desk? The VAT man cometh. Any good at accounts, Olivia?"

"I'm a qualified accountant," said Olivia.

"So what were you doing dogsbodying on a fashion magazine?" asked Agatha.

Olivia shrugged. "I thought it would be glamorous, but it was the pits. Lead me to it."

Agatha reflected guiltily that she had landed lucky with Olivia. Poor Mrs. Freedman was eternally baffled by taxes. Agatha did employ a firm of accountants, but Mrs. Freedman always slowed things up, claiming she was able to do the taxes, so Agatha was often penalised for being late with her returns. In fact, thought Agatha, Mrs. Freedman was not much shakes as a secretary, but as Phil said in his gentle voice, "She useless. But she's *our* useless."

Jake thought Olivia was a reassuring, familiar type. He had attended parties at the London Season and was familiar with the straight blond hair and hunting shoulders of Olivia's type of girl. Also, he was smarting after a sharp put-down from Toni earlier in the day. They had tracked down a missing child and returned the girl to her weeping and grateful parents. Efficient as ever, Toni made sure the local press were there for the handover.

Jake had used the euphoria of the moment to grab hold of Toni and kiss her. He might just have got away with it had he not thrust his tongue down Toni's throat. So in front of the parents and the press, she had told him savagely to never, ever try that again.

The trouble with Jake, a trouble that his father was well aware of, was that Jake plunged into every new job with great enthusiasm, and then suddenly got bored. Aware that his family were very rich indeed and that he did not really need to work, all Jake wanted to do was slope around London. He suddenly missed London. He had done a bit of the Season because his father had hoped a suitable girl would stiffen his spine, but Jake had spent the time getting drunk at balls and parties and capsizing a boat at Henley Regatta. At the end of the day, he offered to run Olivia home. She said regretfully that she had her car.

Still smarting after Toni's rebuff and longing for a bit of female adoration, Jake invited her for dinner. Olivia accepted. She suddenly wished she were in London at her flat so that her friends could see her escorted by this Adonis. But she always went home when she was between jobs. Jake chose a Chinese restaurant although he would have liked to take her to the George but couldn't afford it. Somehow, when they started talking, they both shared a longing to get back to London, and Olivia said she had a flat in Pont Street.

"So what are you doing buried down here?" asked Jake.

"Oh, my parents found out that our neighbour, Charles Fraith, was unmarried. I think they're brokering a deal."

"And you're going along with it? A gorgeous creature like you!" exclaimed Jake.

Olivia could feel her cold retreating as a warm pink glow suffused her body. No one had ever called her gorgeous before.

"Well, you know how it is," said Olivia. "No one else had come along, and the parents were fretting about not having grandchildren and the line dying out and all that yawning stuff. Charles is cute. Mind you, he's a lot older than me, and his mansion is really ugly. He's got a sort of butler, Gustav. Scary. Slab of a Swiss like something out of the Addams Family."

"But you're not engaged?"

"No," said Olivia. "Maybe I'll chuck Agatha's job and go back to London and have a think. Once I'm away from the family, I can think clearer."

"Wish I could go with you," said Jake.

"Why not? I've got a spare room. Gosh! What larks! What will we tell Agatha?"

"Don't need to tell her anything. I got keys to the office. We can go back and leave them on her desk with a note. I'll say I've gone back to Pa, and you can say you're too ill, and your cold has got worse."

"I'll meet you in London. Wait till I scribble the address," said Olivia. "Just wait till my friends see you!"

Agatha read Jake's note in the morning. She thanked her stars she had got him a service flat, to be paid on a weekly basis. She would always think of Jake as That Great Big Red Herring. Of all the red herrings she had encountered, she thought, Jake took the biscuit. Before, all murders had been somehow connected, but not the one of Toby Cross. Then she saw another note from Olivia, cursed, and phoned an agency for a temp.

Then she sat down and scowled horribly. Would they have gone off together? She felt a sudden sharp pang of guilt. She must stop interfering in Charles's life. Although she was sure it was because Olivia's family was rich and Charles, she knew, was mercenary, he had seemed genuine.

She heaved a sigh. She would go and talk to Jenny Coulter again and then go to Harby. There was nothing she could do but keep ferreting away. Mrs. Bull was still in hospital and still protesting that she could not remember anything about her attacker.

She longed to take one of her detectives with her for company, but she had a heavy workload, so after telling Toni to take over and allocate the jobs, Agatha set out to see if Jenny was at home.

Chapter Ten

Jenny was at home. Women like Jenny offended Agatha in an odd way. Why should she, Agatha, diet and spend a fortune at the beauticians to hold the years at bay whereas women like Jenny, opening the door wearing a tracksuit and slippers and shaped like a cottage loaf, saw no reason to bother.

"Oh, it's you again," said Jenny. "But make it quick. My latest is due here soon."

"You mean . . ."

"Yes, dear, so hurry up."

"Can you think of anything at all to help me?"

pleaded Agatha. "Can you think of any little thing? You know Farraday's been murdered?"

"He's no great loss, and his wife is a bitch. I gather from the news this morning he told her where he was going."

"Yes, but she was seen at that sale of work all day," said Agatha.

"Find out how heavily he was insured," said Jenny. "Look, there was nothing in Bellington to arouse sexual passion. It's all about the money. Who stands to gain? Damian. Or the only sexual motive might be because the wife gets back in again with her beloved son. Something of Oedipus about that pair."

Agatha's education on the ancient Greeks was sadly deficient, but no one watching television could avoid having heard of an Oedipus complex. There were even dreadful puns from comedians—"Have you given the Oedipus his milk, dear?"

"Don't let yourself be rushed or pushed," said Jenny. "Go down to that dreadful hall and say you want a room to look through your notes and see if you can pick something up from the atmosphere." All at once, Agatha realised Jenny's charm. She cared about people. She had a strong maternal streak. Smells of fresh coffee and something baking came from the kitchen.

As Agatha left, a man was arriving, a middle-aged business man, expensively tailored and barbered. He had a pleasant face, thinning hair and not much of a paunch. He was carrying a bouquet of a dozen red roses.

When did any man last bring me roses? Agatha fought off a wave of self-pity.

On the dashboard of her car, within reach, was a supply of e-cigarettes, Agatha deciding that if she couldn't stop, less was at least better, and if she smoked fake cigarettes when she was driving, then maybe she might come to prefer them.

Chapter Eleven

U sually one associates blazing autumn colours with somewhere like New England, not the British Isles, but the trees and hedgerows were blazing scarlet gold, purple and even green, the oak trees being the last to turn. Agatha thought gloomily that there was something almost frightening in all this beauty. Would people one day be saying, "Do you remember that glorious autumn we had right before World War Three?"

Her thoughts got gloomier. What happens after death? Are we recycled? What if it should turn out like *Groundhog Day*, and just before you were reborn, you would know that you were being sent back the same person again into the same background to see if you did any better the next time around?

I wouldn't be ambitious, went her thoughts. I'd find a decent fellow and have children. Oh, yeah? said a voice in her head. With your track record, you wouldn't know a decent fellow if he leapt out of your soup and bit you on the bum.

Agatha saw the sign that said HARBY approaching. She wished with all her heart that Damian would sack her. For the first time in her career, Agatha felt defeated. It would be wonderful to leave it to the police. But she sighed as she turned in at the gates leading to the hall.

Agatha's dress betrayed her feelings. She was wearing thick black tights with low heeled ankle boots, black trousers, black sweater and a dark green Barbour. She parked at the front of the hall and hesitated before she rang the bell. What did they do all day? Damian usually looked as if he did nothing. Andrea, when not plunging her hairy body in the pool, was off on some wildlife venture. Their mother flitted here and there, looking busy, but not actually doing anything.

Agatha finally rang the bell. Damian answered the door himself. "Any news?"

"No. I wanted to sit in the hall and go through my

notes so that you could all be on hand if I think of asking something I may have overlooked. I know you've got loads of spare rooms untouched by the human duster."

"Yes, lot of them are locked up. Better find one where the central heating still works. I know. There's one at the end of the west corridor where we keep some junk. Don't scowl. It's got heat and a chair."

The wind whistled round the hall. Agatha looking out a window saw the rising wind sending multicoloured leaves flying off the trees. "Here you are," said Damian, pushing open a door and switching on the light. "Have fun." He went off, whistling.

The room was lit by one dusty naked light bulb which swung in a draught from a badly fitted window. Crowded into the room were many animals and birds in glass cases. There was one battered leather armchair. Stacked along one wall were paintings in ornate frames. Like most of the public who watch the *Antiques Roadshow*, Agatha was persuaded that she would recognise a real master if she saw it. She began to tilt the paintings forward to examine them. But they were all dirty and looked like badly executed family portraits, none of which was recognisable as any of the Bellingtons. Probably, thought Agatha, they had belonged to the previous owners of the hall, who had left them behind with all the Victoriana in the shape of all those creatures under glass.

She opened up her iPad and began to read through all her notes. The wind outside was growing in strength. The light above flickered but stayed on. Agatha shivered, despite the fact that the room was fairly warm. There was something unnerving about all those glass eyes, staring and staring out of their glass prisons. She was about to continue going over her notes when her eye caught a movement over on the wall behind the stacks of paintings. Because of the shadows, she had not noticed it before. It was a dusty greyish-white curtain, the colour of the walls, and it was slowly moving in a draught. Like a child looking for any excuse not to do homework, Agatha got to her feet and began to drag the paintings aside. That achieved she tried to pull aside the curtain until she saw it had simply been nailed to a strip of wood. She lifted the curtain to one side and looked in. There was nothing in the alcove but an old-fashioned Bath wheelchair. It was one of those she had seen in old prints of the town of Bath where invalids went to take the waters. It was made of basket work, a long seat lined with faded and tattered plum-coloured silk. It had a long handle at the front for the invalid to hold on to, or to enable it to be pulled from the front, and a big one at the back for pushing. Agatha shrugged. This wasn't getting her anywhere.

Back to the notes. "*Wooooo!*" screamed the wind, making her jump.

She settled back in her chair and began to read. The voice of her ex-husband sounded in her brain. "The trouble with you, Agatha," she remembered James saying, "is that you solve your cases by ending up a sort of tethered goat. The murderer realises you are on to him, and he decides to bump you off."

What do the other private detectives do? wondered Agatha. Probably leave murders to the police and stick to divorces, missing people, missing dogs and cats and don't end up in a draughty hall with a feeling of failure.

When she got to the bit in her notes about Mrs. Bull ending up down the well, she suddenly twisted round and looked thoughtfully at that alcove. What if the murderer wasn't a big powerful man but an ordinary-sized person? Something like that Bath chair could be used to transport a body. She got up again, slowly cleared the paintings which were blocking the alcove to the other side of the room and wheeled the chair out, putting on a pair of latex gloves first. No use looking for blood. She was drugged. She should phone Bill, get a forensic team to look at it. But Bill would have to tell Wilkes, and Wilkes would say she was fantasising, because he was a snob and did not want to believe the upper classes capable of murder.

"What the hell are you doing?"

Agatha jumped nervously and straightened up from her examination of the chair. Lady Bellington stood framed in the doorway, one hand resting high up on the jamb as if posing for a Russell Flint painting.

"Just examining this old chair," said Agatha.

"That chair and everything else in this room is going off to auction next week. What is it to you?"

"I was thinking about Mrs. Bull. It could have been used to transport her body to the well. Damian told me to use this room to . . ."

"Just get out of my house!"

"What's up?" Damian's voice sounded from behind his mother.

"This creature is poking around."

"I'm paying the creature to poke around. Leave her alone. Wait a minute. What are you doing with that Bath chair, Agatha? Planning your retirement?"

"It could have been used to cart Mrs. Bull to the well."

"What an imagination you do have. But my belief in your reputation is beginning to wear thin. I'll give you one more week."

"Honestly, darling," jeered his mother, "you sound like a TV drama, except on TV, the detective is only given twenty-four hours. She's bound to solve it now! As if."

Her tinkling laugh echoed back as she walked off. I hate women with tinkling laughs, thought Agatha.

"I'll leave you to it." Damian glided out.

"Can I take this chair with me?"

"Got a big enough car?"

"I can put it on the roof rack."

"It is a valuable antique and it's raining like hell."

"Okay, I'll rent a small van," said Agatha. "I'll get it to a private lab and see if Mrs. Bull's DNA is anywhere about."

"If you must."

Agatha drove back to Mircester where she rented a small van. She phoned Toni to tell her what she was doing and asked her to find out if Mrs. Bull was still in hospital, try to get a visit and pinch something with her DNA on it. It was only when she had rung off that Agatha realised how much she depended on Toni.

Agatha should have asked about all the electronic devices and how they worked before driving off. She went down a narrow one-way street in Mircester, and, because it was a dull stormy day, tried to switch the sidelights on and found she had switched on the windscreen washer by mistake and people on the pavement on either side were shouting at her.

As she approached Harby, she began to feel like the amateur detective that Wilkes damned her as. If the Bath chair were a valuable clue, and *if* someone in the castle were responsible for the murders, then a murderer might be waiting for her. Fireworks burst in the night sky, reminding Agatha it was the fifth of November, celebrating the time that Guy Fawkes had tried to burn down the Houses of Parliament.

At the gates of Harby Hall, the lodge keeper came out and handed Agatha a slip of paper. "That be me phone number," he said. "Next time you do be a-coming, phone me and give me a time. I can't be running in and out for the likes o' you."

"What an old charmer you are," said Agatha. But she took the slip of paper and drove on. As she approached the house, a firework shot up over the building and sent a scarlet fountain of red stars to light the sky. The car park was full of cars. Agatha cursed. They must be having a party. No one came to answer the door. She guessed they must be all out in the garden. She tried the handle. The door was not locked. Good, thought Agatha. I can get that chair and disappear with it. She had forgotten which room the chair was in and ran along the corridors opening and shutting doors, wondering why on earth there were so many small rooms on the ground floor. At last she found the right room. She switched on the light and hurried to the alcove, pulled aside the curtain and let out an exclamation of dismay. For the alcove was empty.

Grimly, Agatha marched along the corridor and out

into the garden to the sound of whooshing rockets and cheers. All she could see at first on the terrace was a line of backs silhouetted against some light coming from the garden. Then she smelt smoke. A dreadful idea shot into her mind. Ignoring protests, she elbowed her way to the front. A great bonfire was blazing away. On top of it was perched the 'guy,' a stuffed dummy sitting in that very Bath chair that Agatha so desperately wanted. "No," she cried. "Damian, put the fire out. I need that chair."

She ran forward and was halted by the immense heat from the bonfire. She gazed upwards. The dummy was alight, and the basket work of the chair was covered in flickering flames.

Damian pulled her back. "Who put the chair up there?" panted Agatha.

"Blessed if I know," he said. "I never even noticed it was the old chair you wanted until I heard you shouting."

"Find out for me," said Agatha wearily.

"I'll get you some mulled wine, you old party-pooper," said Damian. "Find yourself somewhere to sit."

Guests were beginning to find seats on bales of straw placed in a circle around the fire. Agatha retreated dismally to a seat at the back of the terrace. Damian handed her a mug of mulled wine. "I'll find out from

Giles Bennet, the factor. He organises the thing every year."

After he had gone, Agatha cautiously sniffed the wine. Then she saw, on a white-clothed table on the terrace, a coffee machine. She poured her mulled wine into the flower pot and decided to have a cup of coffee instead.

She took an e-cigarette out of her pocket and puffed away, swore, put it back in her pocket, pulled out a packet of Bensons, and lit up. Bliss! Unreformed, unholy bliss, thought Agatha.

Damian appeared with Giles. Said Damian, "Giles says he had left the dummy on an old kitchen chair at the back of the bonfire and told the gardener to get a ladder and put it on the top. The gardener says when he went round to the back, there was no chair. The wheel-chair was in the hall and Dinky said, they could take it. He said it was awkward getting it up there, and they had to ask the under gardener to bring another ladder so they could carry it up between them. That was a valuable antique."

"Only you and your mother knew I was coming for it and why," said Agatha.

"Here's Mother. Let's ask her. Did you give that Bath chair to be used on the bonfire?"

"No, I didn't. Oh, dear, that tiresome little woman is back again."

"Did you tell anyone else?" asked Agatha.

"Only the housekeeper. I told her to leave it out by the front door so you could collect it."

"I would like to talk to the housekeeper," said Agatha.

Damian went off. Agatha had a sudden paroxysm of coughing. She stubbed out her cigarette. It couldn't be the cigarette. Must be the smoke from the bonfire.

Damian came back, leading a small, aggressive-looking middle-aged woman. "I ain't done nothing wrong, me lord," she said in a high complaining voice. Of course, thought Agatha. Damian inherited the title.

"Just tell the nice lady what happened, Dinky," said Damian, "and do get on with it. We're missing the party."

"Well, me lady says as how I was to leave the chair outside on the step because a lady would be coming for it. Fred, the gardener, he came in looking for an old chair. 'Wot about yon on the step?' says he. 'Some lady's coming for that,' says I. 'Better leave it,' says he."

Agatha said, "Damian. I really do need to speak to your gardener."

"Well, make it quick."

Agatha lit another cigarette and was immediately assailed by another bout of coughing. The spectre of lung cancer rose up to haunt her. Bollocks, thought

Agatha fiercely, old Mr. Dent smoked twenty a day for years and years and he died aged ninety. But she stubbed the cigarette out.

Damian arrived with the gardener, a surly Scotsman wearing a shiny blue suit. "I telt his lordship, missus," said Fred. "There was a note on that wheelchair saying, 'For charity.' So I chapped at the door and Dinky answered it. I asked if we could take that dirty old chair because a note says it was for charity and like I said, charity begins at home." Agatha waited impatiently until his fit of cackling at his own wit had subsided. "So the housekeeper, she said that it was probably meant for Oxfam or one of those, but it was getting late so just take the damn thing. So I did."

"Do you still have that note?" asked Agatha.

"I did hae it but I chucked it on the fire."

"Someone in this house didn't want me to have that chair," said Agatha.

"Either stay for the party or go home," said Damian. "I do have guests, you know."

"I'll leave," said Agatha. She turned one more time and looked back. A man in a chef's hat was handing out plates of barbecued meat to the guests as they sat round the bonfire.

As Agatha looked, an especially large flame shot up, lighting up the faces of the guests, and there, almost on the other side of the bonfire and nearly out of sight, was Jenny Coulter and her latest beau. Agatha almost went in search of Damian, but decided to phone him the next day and ask him why he had invited his father's ex-mistress.

She drove the van back to Mircester and paid for it, keeping the receipt to put on her expenses for Damian.

Agatha got into her own car and drove home. The lights were on in the living room, and Charles's car was parked outside. She fought down a feeling of gladness.

Charles, as ever, was asleep on the sofa with the cats asleep beside him. He was awakened by Agatha pouring herself a large gin. "Getting to be an addict?" he asked.

Agatha swung round. "I am sick to death of moralisers. I think about giving up smoking, and some scientist tells me that I can't eat bacon, fizzy drinks, cake, have a wood fire because of carbon monoxide and on it goes so I think, What the hell? Put it on my tombstone: 'Here lies Agatha Raisin, late of this parish, nagged to death.'"

"Sorry. Pour me a whisky."

"Your girlfriend has walked out on me."

"I gather she has gone to London with Jake. Didn't manipulate that one, did you?"

"If she'd really wanted to marry you, she'd still be around. Do you know, if you still want her, you can have her, because she'll be back. Okay, she's rich, and

Jake only has money that his father allows. But I think he's a butterfly. I think boredom sets in very quickly with that one after the first tide of enthusiasm has drawn back."

"Talk about something else. My drink? Ta. Any breakthroughs?"

Agatha sat down and told him about the burnt wheelchair.

"Let's see," said Charles. "Let's concentrate on the family and the ex-mistress. Maybe old Ma Bull was right, and Lady Bellington was down in the cellars with a syringe. Damian hires you to cover his tracks. Andrea thinks she'll get money when her dad kicks the bucket, and finds out that Damian has the lot."

Agatha sat slowly down beside him on the sofa. "She accused her brother of being the murderer. There's something else."

She pulled her iPad out of her capacious handbag, switched it on, and began to scroll through her notes. "Here's something. She's wildlife and animal mad. She wanted to open a sanctuary for donkeys, and Damian refused to give her the money. She looks like a change-ling. Damian is languid and beautiful, the mother is elegant in a wasted way, and the unfortunate Andrea looks like a hairy troll."

"Probably takes after father."

"Forgot about that." She stared at Charles, who reflected that when Agatha had one of her flashes of intuition, a gold light shone in her eyes. "Some of these animal libbers can be savage. I can't see her loving the donkeys on her own. Say she teams up with one of the more feral animal libbers. I've always had a feeling there are two people in this."

"So Damian could be next," said Charles. "How did Farraday die?"

"Wait a moment." Agatha phoned Patrick and asked him for news of Farraday's death. When she rang off, she told Charles, "He says he's just heard that Farraday was injected with Oblivon. I remember that drug. It turned up in my second murder case. It's used by vets to tranquillise horses before an operation, but it's instantly lethal to humans. So silly Nigel Farraday got himself killed because he wanted revenge on me."

"Are you going to follow Andrea?"

"I've a feeling she would spot me whatever the disguise. I know, I'll get Simon to check out some hunt saboteurs' meetings. It's that time of year."

"Tell him to go into Mircester University and look at the notice boards. They used to offer students forty pounds plus a packed lunch and transport. Probably still do."

"She might not be at one of those," said Agatha.

"But here are some photos of her that we got from glossy magazines. If she's not there, we'll try something else."

Simon accepted the assignment eagerly. He had been feeling silly. He felt Toni despised him for chasing Alice. The fact that Alice was devoted to Bill Wong had finally cracked the shell of his obsession.

The next day, he went to the university, mingled with the students and studied the noticeboard. And right in the middle of one of them was a poster for Hunt the Hunt. His eyes flicked through all the bit about killing foxes being cruel and got to the bit where fifty pounds, a packed lunch and transport were offered to anyone caring to fight the good fight on on Saturday at Mirton Wold Manor where the hunt was to meet. Coach to leave the abbey car park at eight in the morning. To register phone 0333400691.

Simon left the college, sat in his car, and phoned the number. A girl answered, but it was not Andrea. She had a local accent and gave her name as Tanya. Simon gave his name as Simon Andrews and his job as a checker-out at a supermarket. She demanded his reason for wanting to go. Simon said that he needed the money and would like a day out. Also, he didn't mind a bit of a punch up. She laughed and told him she would see him at the bus on Saturday.

Of course. Saturday is tomorrow, Simon realised.

In the morning, he climbed aboard the bus wearing a black sweater and trousers under a camouflage jacket. Tanya turned out to be a small chubby girl with red hair and freckles. She welcomed Simon with a grin and said, "Most of this lot are here for the money, but you're the only honest one."

Simon took a seat next to a pallid girl with a long white face and bitten nails. "Terrible about them foxes," she said.

"I'm just here for the money," said Simon.

When Simon was not in the grip of one of his obsessions, he was a good detective. He had guessed that most of the turnout would come for the money, and he didn't want to engage in any violence.

But his new companion looked shocked. "That's dreadful. I'll tell Tanya."

"She knows," said Simon. "But she needs the numbers. I mean one of you must be filming."

"Jerry does that. He's got a car."

She turned away in disgust and stared out of the window.

When they reached the manor, they stopped outside the gates. Tanya took a group photo of them all. There was a short drive so that they were able to see the hunt assembled on the lawn outside. They all climbed down from the bus. Simon shouldered his way to the gates, took out a camera and zoomed in on the hunters. He didn't know if Charles hunted but didn't want to risk being noticed. Suddenly, he thought he saw the small figure of Andrea riding a tall hunter. He retreated away from the others and covertly studied the pictures of Andrea he had brought with him. Just to be sure, he climbed up the wall and sat on top of it to get a better look.

She was wearing a pink coat. He had once wondered why scarlet hunting jackets were called 'pink,' had looked it up and found they were named after a tailor called Pink who had bought too much scarlet cloth for army uniforms and had been left with a surplus and so had created the hunting coat.

Stirrup cups were being handed up to the riders. Andrea scowled and refused the drink.

"Get down off that wall," shouted a voice below Simon.

Simon twisted around. A tall policeman, one of many, had just arrived.

Scrabbling down the wall and joining the others, Simon wished he'd worn a balaclava over his face like some of the others. He hoped none of the policemen would recognise him.

Two men swung the gates open. The hounds trotted out, the horsemen followed. And then the Master of the Hunt clasped his chest and said, "I'm sick. Get an ambulance." Riders dismounted and helped him down.

Then others of the hunt were dismounting and vomiting. Then Simon saw Bill Wong giving instructions. Bill saw Simon and scowled, but Simon held a finger to his lips and mimed he had to talk to him. So Bill got two policemen to drag Simon behind a police van and demanded, "Make it look good."

"Andrea Bellington is from Harby Hall," said Simon. "She's into animal rights. She refused the stirrup cup which is why she's about the only one not being sick. Get whatever bottles supplied the stirrup cup and get it analysed."

"Right. Thanks, Simon. Now bugger off." He said to the two policemen who had brought Simon, "Throw him back."

Members of Hunt the Hunt looked on sympathetically as Simon was carried up to join them and thrown on the ground. They all began to shout about police brutality with the exception of Tanya, who was on her mobile phone saying, "Well, if the hunt is cancelled, they can have their lunch but no pay."

Simon could hear the wail of approaching sirens. He managed to ease up to the gate and looked down the drive. Andrea was standing by her horse and speaking rapidly into a mobile phone.

Andrea rang off and looked in surprise as Bill Wong and two policemen approached her, and then all three went into the manor.

It was a long day for Simon. All the would-be sabo-teurs had to be interrogated and their names and finger-prints taken. Warned beforehand by Bill Wong, the policeman who interviewed Simon accepted his fake name and fake address without a murmur.

He decided to find out if any of them knew Andrea. He did not ask outright but wondered out loud whether Hunt the Hunt had someone on the inside. Some looked blank, others said they had seen a lot of children running around the grounds of the manor, and it was probably one of them who had decided to play a trick. Tanya shouted that they would drive on and look for another hunt. Simon's bus companion, the pallid girl, volunteered that her name was Flossie. Simon realised that Flossie was one of the genuine protestors and asked her if Hunt the Hunt had a mole.

"You mean someone on the inside?" asked Flossie.

"Yes."

"'Scuse me."

"Where are you going?" demanded Simon, but standing up to let her past him for she had been sitting in the seat at the window.

"Going to have a piss. Okay?"

"Sure."

It was then that Simon realised that the bus did not have a toilet, and Flossie was bent over Tanya, who was seated at the back of the bus, and speaking urgently.

Then Tanya leaned across the aisle and whispered to two thuggish-looking men with shaven heads and face piercings.

This could get nasty, thought Simon. He started to make retching noises and called to the driver, "Stop the bus. I'm going to be sick." The driver slammed on the brakes, and Simon hurtled off the bus and into nearby woods, running as hard as he could when he heard the sounds of pursuit. At last he rolled into a hollow, covered himself with piles of dead leaves, and waited anxiously. He heard the sound of many voices and realised the whole coachload had turned out to find him. Voices cried, "Kill the bastard." Simon shivered, reflecting that although they were against cruelty to animals, there was nothing in their minds to stop them being cruel to people.

What possibly saved him was the fact that most of the coachload only wanted a paid day out. He heard them finally returning to the bus, complaining to Tanya that he was long gone. Soon he heard the bus move off and slowly sat up. A large dog fox regarded him solemnly before slinking away.

Agatha's eyes gleamed when Simon reported his day. "That's great news," she said. "Now, we're getting somewhere."

"How can we pin it on Andrea?" asked Simon.

"Don't you see? Farraday was killed by Oblivon. So

if this emetic turns out to be something you give to animals, it means we can start looking for a vet. Patrick, see how quickly you can find out what was in the stirrup cup."

"This isn't *CSI Miami*," grumbled Patrick. "Could take a week."

"Well, see if she was the only one who refused the stirrup cup."

"I doubt it. I think half the world's been in rehab."

"Oh, *Patrick*," exclaimed Agatha. "Just do it."

By the following day, Patrick had found out that three other members of the hunt had refused the stirrup cup. One because it was port and said the stuff served was filth and the other two, recovering alcoholics. Andrea said she didn't drink cheap booze and that's what the folk at the manor always served.

"I want you, Patrick and Phil, to follow Andrea. Could you wear different footwear, Patrick? These black shoes and socks mark you out as a copper. See if she knows a vet. Of course, if she has a horse, it stands to reason she knows a vet."

After her two detectives had gone off, Agatha was just about to go out on a case that Patrick had been working on when the door of the office opened and Damian strolled in.

"What's happened?" asked Agatha.

He took a chair on the other side of her desk. He's going to turn it round and lean his arms on the back, thought Agatha, and that is what Damian did.

"I've come to pay my bill," he said.

"But we're still working on it," protested Agatha.

"I don't want to be rude, dear lady, but I have come to the conclusion that you're a waste of space. Give me my bill."

"Are we getting too close to home?" asked Agatha.

"Just shut up, and I'll pay up."

Agatha was suddenly glad that the elderly temp was at her desk in the corner. Mrs. Freedman was still poorly, and Agatha had phoned the agency and demanded the oldest secretary they had on their books. She was called Harriet Teller, grey-haired, thick glasses, tweedily dressed.

"Harriet," said Agatha, "add up the expenses so far and give Lord Bellington the bill."

"Certainly," said Harriet. "It will only take a few minutes."

Agatha studied Damian. Despite the effeminacy of his face, there was something masculine about his deep voice and strong body.

"Stop staring," said Damian languidly. "It's rude."

"I'm wondering why you want me to stop investigating," said Agatha.

"Because you are useless. Will that do?"

"No, it won't. I have a good success rate. Did you hire me because you thought I was useless?"

"This is boring. Give me the damned bill."

Harriet brought it over. He glanced at it, drew out a chequebook and signed it. He stood up and said, "Don't come near the hall or any of my family."

"What did you make of him, Harriet?" asked Agatha.

"Anxious and frightened," said Harriet.

"Now, that's sharp of you. I think it has something to do with his sister."

"This is hopeless," said Phil. "Here we are in Harby and highly conspicuous. We can't lurk outside the hall or the lodge keeper will report us. There isn't a pub in this village."

"Let's find out the nearest one," said Patrick. "There must be somewhere for the locals. I'll ask that old codger over there." He got out of the car and came back to say, "The Prince of Wales is down that road to the left."

"Another village?"

"No, one of those places stuck out in the country-side."

They found the pub and noticed there were quite a few vehicles in the car park. "We can hardly go in there and start questioning people," said Phil.

"We can listen to gossip. I mean, it's been all over the newspapers. We can say we read about it. Also, we can ask about a vet. We'll find someone chatty."

"What shall we say we do?" asked Phil.

"We could say we're travelling salesmen," said Patrick.

Phil said, "Won't do. I'd then have to think what I was selling and why I was in this neck of the woods. Just say we're pals and retired."

They reached the pub and collected their drinks. Two people had just vacated an old-fashioned settle by the fire. They sat down and looked hopefully at two old men in the settle facing them.

Phil said, "Is there a vet near here?"

Two old faces stared at him without blinking. Phil wondered if they were brothers. Both were wearing woollen caps, both had grey stubble and weak blue watery eyes.

What it is to be a detective, thought Patrick. Instead of saying, Get stuffed, I have to say, "I see your glasses are empty. Like a drink?"

"Oh, ar, very kind of you, I'm sure," said one. "That'll be two pints."

While Patrick went to get the drinks, one of the men said, "I'm Cedric and this 'ere is brother, Tom. You was asking about a vet? Well, thank ee kindly," as Patrick put two pints of beer on the table in front of them. "That ud be young Henry Jessop over at Orlington Sudbury. Got trouble?"

"My cat, Daisy, is poorly," said Phil. "Got her in the car."

"If you go out and drive to the left, you'll come to a crossroads and you'll see the sign to Orlington Sudbury. The vet's is on the village green," said Tom.

"Want another pint?" asked Phil.

"Surely. Very kind."

Phil went to the bar this time. He and Patrick were sticking to soft drinks.

"Over our way," said Patrick, "there's was a vet once who was a terror with the ladies."

The two brothers began to chortle and nudge each other. "What's so funny?" asked Patrick.

"Henry the vet, see, he's been way of courting Miss Andrea from the hall," said Tom.

"So what's funny about that?" asked Patrick as Phil came back with the drinks. He told Phil what Tom had just said.

"Cos Miss Andrea do have a temper. Henry was chatting to a young miss outside his office, and Andrea turns up like the wrath of God and slaps that poor girl and sends her running," said Cedric. "Better'n them soaps on the telly."

"Do they plan to marry?" asked Patrick.

"No," said Cedric. "See, Henry don't want to, but

she'll make him, and that's a fact. She's Lord Bellington's sister, see, and she feels that gives her the right to throw her weight around."

Patrick and Phil decided to move on, Phil, once they were outside, wondering at the strength of the brothers' bladders. "I could never hold that amount of beer without rushing to the toilet," he said.

"Let's find Orlington Sudbury. If it's got a pub, I wouldn't mind a half of beer and a steak and kidney pie," said Patrick. "Have you got a photo of this Andrea?"

"Only ones out of magazines, hunt balls, that sort of thing. But she's small and angry-looking. I think I can recognise her."

Orlington Sudbury turned out to be a large village. It had a sprawling council estate on the outskirts, and then the road twisted and wound through the village. Probably followed a drove road in the olden days, thought Phil. But the village green was there, the pub looking pretty with flowers in the window boxes. It was called the Living End.

"Odd name for a pub," said Patrick.

"With a name like that," said Phil, "it's probably being run by some retired chap who thinks he can run a pub, and all he does is drink the profits. If they've any food it'll probably be listed on a twee menu."

Two surprises hit them when they walked in. Mine host was a Chinese gentleman, in a white shirt and black jacket and trousers. And seated over in a corner was a woman Phil was sure was Andrea with a good-looking man.

Well, he would have been good-looking, thought Phil, taking another covert glance, if he hadn't been a bit weak about the mouth. To their dismay, the pub started filling up, until standing drinkers blocked their view of Andrea and who they believed might be the vet.

"I'll take a look," said Patrick. He got up and, being tall, was able to see Andrea and the man leaving. The man was protesting, and Andrea was arguing. Patrick shouldered his way through the crowd to the window and looked out. Andrea got in a car and drove off. The man watched her go and trailed off into a door with a brass plate on the other side off the green.

He returned to Phil. "The landlord says that the vet is the other side of the green," said Phil, "and I ordered steak and kidney pie for both of us."

"That's where Andrea's chap went," said Patrick.

"What should we do now?" asked Phil. "Charge in there and accuse him of providing Andrea with poison?"

"I'll think better when I've eaten," said Patrick.

The pie was the best they had ever tasted.

"It's like this," said Patrick, "we'd better tell Agatha what we've found out. Let's pay the bill and go outside where it's quiet and no one can hear us."

There was a pond in the middle of the village

green. A mallard sailed across, leaving a V in the water behind it.

"The pub could do with a car park," said Patrick. Their car was blocked in by other cars parked at the front. "We'll go to that bench on the far side of the pond and have a think."

"I'll phone Agatha," said Phil.

Patrick heard Phil tell Agatha about the vet and then heard the excited squawking of Agatha's voice in reply but could not make out the words.

"Well?" he asked when Phil rang off.

"She says she's coming here right away."

"What! Andrea knows what she looks like. If she's got any of that Oblivon left, one drop of it could be the end of Agatha."

"And she says we're to clear off!"

"I don't think she knows what she's doing. She's been down in the mouth lately. And when she's depressed, she starts to daydream. She's probably imagining newspaper headlines of how she solved the case."

"Tell you what we can do," said Phil. "It'll be dark by the time she gets here. We'll wait down the road as soon as we can get to our car and watch for her. Then all we have to do is follow her."

Chapter Twelve

As Agatha was hurrying from the office, she bumped into Charles. "Have you seen Olivia?" he asked.

"She disappeared the same day as Jake. Work it out," snapped Agatha.

"Which is what you planned," said Charles. "Where are you off to?"

"Mind your own business," shouted Agatha. "I am working. I am about to solve these murders. So why don't you push off and find yourself another deb whose family has pots of money?" The fact that Charles had asked about Olivia had brought all Agatha's feelings of worthlessness back.

Her eyes were bright with unshed tears. She brushed past him and walked to her car.

Charles made his way up to Agatha's office. Toni was there. He asked her if she knew where Agatha had was going.

"She said she was going to Orlington Sudbury." Charles wondered whether he should go after her. The hell with Agatha, thought Charles bitterly. Let her cope with her own mess for once. Why had she turned nasty again?

Agatha had not stopped to consider the wisdom of what she was doing. She was furious with the idea that Damian may have considered her incompetent and had only hired her because he guessed his sister to be guilty. Also, the episode with Jake still hurt.

It was late when she got to Orlington Sudbury, but she saw the pub was open, welcome lights from its windows reflected in the village pond. There was no light on at the vet's. Agatha had located the surgery on the other side of the pond. She suddenly wished she had asked Patrick and Phil to wait for her, not knowing the pair of them had seen her arrive. They had parked behind a stand of trees at the entrance to the village.

She decided to go to the pub and see if she could

pick up any gossip. The dinner hour was over, and there were only a few drinkers in the dim lights of the pub's lamps. And then Agatha saw Gerald Devere, sitting at a table by the window, looking across to the vet's surgery.

"Oh, it's you," he said sulkily. "Shove off. I've got the vet coming to have a drink with me, and I don't want him frightened off."

"No, I will not shove off," said Agatha. "I worked it all out. Obviously you did the same thing."

"You are not muscling in on my table. Go away!"

"Why haven't you called the police?" asked Agatha.

"Because it's time you country clodhoppers learned from a decent detective. Go away!"

Agatha hesitated only a moment. Then she walked straight out of the pub and right over to the veterinary surgery and rang the bell. The name on the brass plate beside the door said, HENRY JESSOP, VETERINARY SURGEON.

Had Gerald still been watching the surgery from the pub, he would certainly have run after her, but he was distracted by some old gypsy tugging at his sleeve. "White heather, mister," she said in a cracked voice. She smelled awful. Gerald shouted to the owner. "Get her away from me."

The owner hurried over and propelled the old woman out of doors.

When Gerald returned to his vigil, there was no sign of Agatha. He did not know that, getting no answer when she rang the bell and seeing a light on inside, she had decided to search round the back. He had felt very clever at joining the clues of Oblivon with a vet and Andrea's love of animals. Now he felt put out that Agatha had come to the same conclusion.

He took a gulp of his drink. It dawned on him that Agatha had probably gone straight to the vet to steal a march on him. He tried to get to his feet, but his legs had no strength. He slowly sank to the floor and drifted off into unconsciousness.

The landlord phoned for an ambulance.

Agatha, in the darkness of the back of the vet's, felt her phone vibrate. She glanced at the dial. Patrick. She whispered into the phone. "I'm at the vet's, but don't come yet. Gerald Devere is in the pub. See if you can distract him."

She tried the handle of a door at the back. Locked. What if he were lying there dead? What if Andrea had learned that he was about to talk to Gerald and had finished him off? If she were in the police force, thought Agatha, she could have claimed to have heard what sounded like a scream and break a glass panel on the door. But being a veterinary surgery with drugs inside, it probably had a sophisticated burglar alarm system. Wait a bit. He surely didn't live in the place. Where was his home?

She walked back round the front and jumped as a man's voice said, "Are you looking for Mr. Jessop?"

Agatha swung round. A tall thin man stood there, leaning on a stick. "Yes," said Agatha. "Do you know where he lives?"

"Yes, but he's not on duty this evening. In fact he's gone off to the disco in Mircester with Penny, my daughter."

"Do you know which disco?"

"You must be desperate. But you'll just have to wait until the morning. I am not going to spoil my daughter's night out." He walked off just as Agatha's phone vibrated.

"What is it, Patrick?" she whispered.

"Gerald's been taken off in an ambulance."

"I didn't hear a siren."

"Wasn't one. Ambulance men must have thought they were picking up a drunk."

"Try to find out what happened to him. Our vet is in Mircester. I'm going there."

Once in Mircester, Agatha phoned Toni and asked her to name a likely disco.

"There's only two. The most popular is the Rooba in Abbey Lane. Want me to come with you?"

"No. Well, maybe." Agatha told her what it was about.

"I'd better go," said Toni. "Someone of your age barging in and asking questions might put the wind up him." Agatha winced. "I'll get Simon, and we'll both go. What does this vet look like?"

"Haven't seen him."

"What's his name?"

"Henry Jessop."

"I'll see if there's anything on the Internet before I start searching for him. What are we asking him?"

"Ask him if he knows Andrea Bellington and see his reaction. Take it from there."

"Where will you be?"

"Phone me when you get the right disco, and I'll wait outside in my car."

When she had rung off, Agatha took out her iPad to see if she could find a photograph of Henry herself. There was nothing there. She tried Andrea. Some photographs, one with a fairly good-looking man. She phoned Patrick. "What does Henry look like?"

"Fairly handsome but weak chin, brown hair, medium height, but pointy ears like Dr. Spock."

"Right. What about Gerald?"

"I'll try my police contacts as well."

Agatha rang off and then rang Toni and passed on

the description. "I think I have it," said Toni. "Hunt ball last year with Andrea."

Toni and Simon tried the Rooba first. They gyrated their way around the dance floor, always studying the faces shining in the lights from the revolving crystal ball over the floor. The music stopped. A voice behind Toni said, "Sorry, Penny, I'd better take this."

Toni drew Simon aside and said, "That's him. Going to the gents. He's taking a phone call."

Simon sped off. He nearly bumped into Henry, who was just inside the door, speaking on his mobile. Better pretend to pee, thought Simon, and it'll have to be pretend because I don't feel like it.

"I don't think we should be seen together for a while," Henry was saying. "In fact, I'm due leave. I'll go abroad. What? Don't threaten me. What? Damned music. Can't hear a thing." For the disco music had started up again and was piped into the toilets.

Toni was sitting on a stool at the bar with Penny, having complained of being thirsty and having invited Penny for a drink. Penny had initially stared at her blankly and rudely and had turned away, so Toni went to the bar alone. To her surprise, she was joined five minutes later by Penny.

"Sorry," she said. "My date seemed to have disappeared."

"What'll you have?"

"Rum and coke."

"Okay." Toni gave the order.

Simon emerged from the toilet, saw Toni over at the bar with Penny, and decided to join them. Henry had disappeared into one of the cubicles. Simon was sure he would join his date when he emerged.

As he approached the bar, he wondered why the fairly handsome Henry had chosen to date this Penny. She was obviously young, in her late teens. She was wearing a glittery sweater across heavy breasts. The pink stripes she had sprayed with an inexpert hand on her blonded hair looked more Hallowe'en than chic. She had a penetrating voice, which was just as well for Toni because the music had started up again. It was a high, arrogant sort of Yah-Yah voice.

"Of course, if we get married, Daddy will be pleased. I mean he's got simply thousands of cattle over at our farm in Belgium and a vet in the family would be useful. Where is he?"

"Is he in the gents?" asked Simon with pretended innocence.

"Oh, this is Simon," said Toni.

"Yes, Henry went there, ages ago."

"I'll go and look," said Simon, suddenly uneasy.

He hurried back, edging his way round the edge of the floor. There were a lot of young men in the toilets.

At the end of the urinals were two cubicles, but both doors were open, showing they were empty.

Phil and Patrick had joined forces with Agatha when Simon called to say that Henry had disappeared from the nightclub after getting a phone call.

"Right," said Agatha. "You may as well go home now, Simon, and tell Toni to do the same."

She turned to Patrick and Phil. "We'll all get into Phil's car. It's the least noticeable. We'll hide near the entrance to Harby Hall."

"Maybe I should wait here," said Patrick.

"All right. I'll go on with it, and we'll phone you if he turns up at the hall."

Phil drove under the shade of a thick stand of trees, which provided enough cover for them despite the fact that most of the leaves had gone.

"He'll need to rouse the lodge keeper," said Phil.

"Yes," replied Agatha. "Odd that, in this day and age. Oh, snakes and bastards! We should have brought two cars.

"There must be another entrance. Say, a tradesman's entrance. I can't see that grumpy old bugger of a lodge keeper leaping out the whole time. In fact, if I were Henry, I wouldn't use this entrance at this time of night. Better call Patrick and get him up here to watch the front entrance instead of us just in case."

Phil started up the car and they cruised slowly,

following the dry stone wall that bordered the estate. "There!" said Agatha, seeing an entrance in the head-lights.

But the bumpy, rutted road led to stables. "Rats!" said Agatha.

"The stables are near the house," Phil pointed out. "If a vet were legitimately visiting, he'd call at the stables."

"You're right." Agatha stared gloomily through the windscreen. "But to go forward, we'll need to get out from under the cover of these trees. There's nothing now in front of us and the stables but grassy fields."

"The stables are in blackness," said Phil. "Nobody to look out at us. We could just walk it, keeping to the side. There's a big cloud coming up to cover the moon. Good time to go."

Agatha groaned inwardly but was glad she had flat shoes on that she used for driving.

"What are we going to do when we get there?" asked Phil.

"See if Henry turns up, see if we can see them together and hear something."

"Circle well away from the stables," said Phil. "They may have security cameras."

"They don't have any. That came out during the investigation."

They crept past the stables. A horse whinnied and

stamped, making them clutch each other. Then they moved on past the stables and towards the bulk of the house.

"How long have we been at Harby?" asked Agatha. "I mean since leaving Patrick."

"Must be at least three-quarters of an hour," replied Patrick.

"Then if he's coming here, he should be here any moment, or if he came in by the front, he could already be here. The trouble is, there are so many rooms in the place, so many small rooms. Odd. It's as if it used to have salons or something, and some mad person got the builders in and had them all cut up."

"Could have been someone with a cottage mentality," said Phil. "Felt overawed by large drawing rooms. We're nearly at the house. We'd better whisper."

"There are lights shining at the back," said Agatha. "It's where there's a terrace overlooking the pool. I've forgotten my tape recorder. Have you got one? Someone might say something incriminating."

And someone might not turn up, thought Phil gloomily. Agatha is *willing* something to happen.

But as they crept up the terrace towards the long windows because one window was slightly open, they could hear a breathless man's voice say, "I came as soon as I could."

Phil switched on the tape recorder.

The same voice again. "What's the panic?"

Andrea's voice. "My dear brother here says if we don't get the hell out of the country, he's going to the police. It's all Father's fault, Damian. He should have given me the money for that donkey sanctuary."

"And I wouldn't give you any either," said Damian. "Was I next?"

"How did you find out?" asked Andrea.

"One of the grooms mentioned you had been using an old room above the stables and wondered if he could rent it. I said I'd take a look at it. I found Oblivon. I found plans for the donkey sanctuary. I found the remains of antifreeze. And if that weren't enough, you put the lot on a computer, you silly cow. I fired that detective. So last chance. I don't want any scandal. Get out the country, and take your precious vet with you."

"She did it all," shouted Henry.

"Oh, yeah? So who gave her the Oblivon?"

Silence.

Then Agatha's leg gave a twinge of cramp. She tried to stand up, staggered and clutched the wall. But her foot dislodged a pebble, which seemed to take an extraordinarily, large noise for such a small piece.

"Someone's out there!" shouted Damian. Agatha and Phil took to their heels and ran.

Then Phil, with surprising strength for an elderly man, suddenly pushed Agatha into some shrubbery and fell on top of her. "We'll never outrun them," he said. "Lie still."

"Okay," muttered Agatha. "But get off me. If we ever get out of here, we'd better go to the police. Wilkes will rave. Tape recordings are not admissible in court. We'll need to hope like hell that Damian didn't destroy the evidence."

"Don't worry," said Phil. "I feel Henry will crack. Shhh! They're quite near."

Damian was giving orders to someone. "Get down to the village and get Tolly's dogs. They'll soon sniff the snooper out."

Agatha crouched, shivering with fear as the voices faded away. "I'm not waiting to be mauled by some Hound of the Baskervilles. Let's get to the main drive and see if Patrick can call the police."

Patrick replied that the lodge gate was open, and that if they could make it to the main drive, he could race in and get them. "Police should be here soon," he said. "They were all over the place before I rushed up here, trying to find out what happened to Gerald."

But Patrick had to wait until several cars from the village roared up the drive. He drove in behind them, assuming they would think he had come from the village to help in the hunt as well.

Agatha and Phil were creeping in what they hoped was the direction of the main drive, because the night had become very black, when the heavens opened and the rain poured down stabbing torrents of icy rain.

They crouched beside the main drive. Cars roared past them. "How will we recognise Patrick's car?" asked Agatha. "Can't see anything but headlights in this pouring rain. This is mediaeval. I think the bastard's roused the whole village to hunt us down."

At last, they saw a flicking of headlights. "Let's risk it!" said Agatha, and jumped out into the middle of the road. At first, she thought she'd made a terrible mistake as the car accelerated towards her, and she threw herself into a bush at the side of the road. But the car stopped and Patrick's voice said urgently, "Get in."

Soaking wet, they dived into Patrick's car. He did a U-turn and raced off. They saw the white face of the lodge keeper as they roared past. "That's torn it," said Patrick. "They'll all be in pursuit."

"For God's sake, man, put your foot down," yelled Agatha. But Patrick continued at a sedate pace and swung down a farm track and finally parked near some trees.

"There!" he said. "I always wonder in movies why, when the villain is chasing the hero, he doesn't just get off the road. I'm sorry I can't put the heater on, Agatha, but we don't want to attract attention."

"All right," said Agatha. "Now, as you are the one with the tape, Phil, you have the honour of phoning

Mircester headquarters. I don't think I could bear to hear Wilkes."

"There are police in the village because of what happened to Gerald. That's a start," said Patrick.

Phil phoned and went through the whole business of being put through several people until he got to Inspector Wilkes. He was told they were all to stay exactly where they were.

Agatha shivered. A dramatic ending, but not that dramatic. For once, there was no Charles to ride to the rescue.

The wail of sirens sounded from the road. "That'll be the lot from the village. Good," said Patrick. "We'll go to the pub and get you dried out."

"It's just after eleven," said Agatha, squinting at the luminous dial of her watch. "They'll be closed."

"They'll be open for the police. I think it's safe to go now."

The landlord said they were welcome to come in. The police had left a short time ago, but he would make up the fire and get them some drinks. Phil phoned to leave a message as to where they could be found.

But just as they were getting warm and dry, there was a call from Wilkes summoning them to the hall and telling them to make sure they had the tape.

They were ushered into the drawing room at the hall, where they found Andrea, Damian and their mother, all looking relaxed and amused. There was no sign of Henry.

"Play the tape," ordered Wilkes.

To Agatha's amazement, the Bellingtons simply looked amused. When the recording was finished, Damian said languidly, "Aren't we convincing? We knew Agatha was outside the window, snooping, so we all decided to give her something worth snooping for. You should see your faces!"

"But you called for help finding us. You called for dogs!" shouted Agatha.

"I'd fired you, sweetie, and I planned to give you the fright of your life. I hope I did."

"Where's Henry?"

"Goner home, I suppose," said Damian. "Dear me, inspector, you are quite red in the face."

"I am taking you all in for questioning," said Wilkes. "All of you!" He turned to his men. "Wong, get two to help you, and bring that vet in to headquarters. You are all to be questioned, and that includes you, Ms. Agatha Raisin!"

Epilogue

The black clouds were rolling away to the east, and an angry red sun was gilding the old jumbled roofs of Mircester when Agatha was finally released from police headquarters. She had driven her own car up from Orlington Sudbury.

She still could not believe it. Wilkes was sure Damian was telling the truth. But where was Henry? Surely the fact that no one had found him pointed to guilt?

Agatha saw the tired figure of Bill Wong emerging and went to join him. "It's a no go," he said. "Damian has even got those villagers who turned up to hunt you down to say it was all a joke. But there's one consolation for you."

"What's that?"

"They've put out an all points bulletin for Henry. He would be the weak link if he didn't actually murder anyone himself."

"If they've left him alive," said Agatha gloomily. "I've an awful feeling we'll never find him now."

Agatha drove slowly home, very tired, and chilled to the bone. Even with the car heater blasting, the chill seemed as if it were lodged inside her forever.

When she arrived outside her cottage and let herself in, she petted her cats and chased them out into the garden before climbing the stairs to look into the spare room. She had hoped perhaps that Charles might be there, but the room was empty.

She had a hot shower and then went to bed, finding herself thinking of Jake and wondering whatever had happened to him.

Jake was feeling trapped. His delight at being back in London had waned because Olivia's father had researched the Lisle family and found Jake's father to be not only respectable but very rich. So he had phoned Mr. Lisle to meet at his club, and it was decided that Jake should study for the stockbroking exams.

The fact that Jake had not even proposed marriage to Olivia was ignored. Olivia said they were close, that they were in love, and that was enough for both fathers. Jake passionately did not want to be a stockbroker, but his father was giving him a generous allowance, and he knew that allowance would be cut off if he said he didn't want to study for the exams.

Also, Olivia liked expensive restaurants. And she expected him to pay half of the rent. He had assumed the flat in Pont Street would be owned by her. Bed was a disappointment. She was surprisingly bony and went so stiff during lovemaking that he felt as if he were romancing a plank.

Sometimes, he thought of Agatha, all curves, passion and French perfume, and wished he had never left the agency. How to escape?

One blessed quiet evening, while Olivia had gone off to a hen party, he put up his feet and turned on the television. *Crime Watch* was showing, and Jake noticed they were still hunting for that vet. Still, his detective days were over, so he switched over to a travelogue on Madeira. As the cold wind howled down Pont Street outside, Jake gazed at scenes of sunshine and wished he were there. I just haven't enough money to escape, he thought. If I were a villain, I could simply go out and mug someone. Then he remembered that he still had the keys to the carpentry shop, and in the office was a safe where

Mr. Bonlieu kept a stack of money, perhaps to pay people off the books. Jake had noticed the money one day when Bonlieu had left the safe open while he berated Jake for laziness. But they would have changed the locks after the murder, wouldn't they? Jake suddenly decided to try.

The last time he had gone in by the back door, it had not been burglar alarmed. He was smiling to find his key still worked when a burglar alarm went off over his head. He hurriedly typed in 1066 in the alarm box, and the shrill noise stopped. It was the same code for the burglar alarm at the front of the shop. Didn't they realise, wondered Jake, that 1066 must be one of the most common security codes in the British Isles? Most school history was forgotten except for the date of the Battle of Hastings.

He made his way through to the office, remembering it was never locked. Now to find the code for the safe. He searched the desk and then remembered he had forgotten to keep his gloves on. The hell with it. He went on searching. Then he wondered, it couldn't possibly be the Battle of Hastings again. He twisted the dial—1066—and grinned as he swung the door open. There were two neat stacks of twenty pounds notes. He took one stack. After closing the safe, he decided not to trouble wiping off his fingerprints. Bonlieu couldn't report the theft to the police in case PC Plod asked if he had declared it on his income tax.

Now, one more night with Olivia!

Jake called in at a travel agent early the following morning and booked a flight to Funchal in Madeira and a room at the famous Reid's palace hotel.

Now, Jake's father had often grumbled that his son was a waste of a first-class brain. As he approached the check-in desk and queued up behind a bearded young man, Jake suddenly felt a frisson of recognition as the young man turned and looked nervously behind him. It was the face he'd seen on crime watch.

Jake did not even pause to think. Throwing his arms around the man and holding him in a tight grip, he shouted, "Henry Jessop! I am making a citizen's arrest!"

The vet struggled free, tried to run but was brought down by a rugby tackle from Jake. Airport security came running.

Agatha watched the morning news on television as she drank her coffee and stiffened in amazement as Jake's handsome face appeared on the screen. He was a hero! He had arrested a man the police were looking for at Heathrow Airport. The report went on to say that Mr. Jake Lisle had been on his way to take a flight to Madeira. What on earth could he be doing going to Madeira, wondered Agatha. And then with one of her flashes of intuition, she realised that Jake was probably running away from Crime Watch.

The police would sweat Henry, and Henry would confess to his involvement. But could Andrea really have killed her own father?

A day later, before she went to the office, she marched into police headquarters and demanded to speak to Bill Wong, only to be told it was his day off. Right, thought Agatha. He no longer lives with his parents. I'll go and see him now.

Bill answered the door, looking sleepy and still wearing his pyjamas. "Come in, Agatha," he said, "but don't ask me about the case. You know I'm not allowed to talk about it."

Agatha plumped herself down on a sofa in Bill's small living room and glared at him. "You lot wouldn't have a case if it hadn't been for me. One thing. Did Henry talk?"

"Okay. But I never told you anything," sighed Bill, slumping down on the sofa next to Agatha. "Yes, Henry told the story. Reading between the lines, it seems as if Henry did not enjoy being a vet. He dated Andrea, and she talked about her dream of a donkey sanctuary somewhere in the Scottish Highlands. They would have a cottage. They would live a blissful Arcadian existence with the dear donkeys. Andrea had become obsessed with the dream. Father wouldn't pay up, so Father had to go. She was shattered when the will was read and she found that apart from an allowance,

Damian got the lot. But Mrs. Bull had overheard her talking to Henry about the murder and had tried to blackmail Andrea, and so Mrs. Bull had to go. Henry was challenged with the fact that Andrea alone could not have put those slabs on top of the well or have chucked the old housekeeper down it without assistance, but Henry insisted she did it alone.

"Farraday had to go, too, because Andrea believed he must know something, or why else would his wife say so at the fair? The only thing that does seem the truth is that Henry really did not like being a vet and, odd in his profession, had an anthropomorphic view of animals and had been hospitalised a view years back for attempted suicide and diagnosed as suffering from acute depression. Wilkes is going to have a go at Andrea later today. I think when she hears just how much he's landing her in it, she might tell us the truth about his involvement."

But later that day, Patrick told Agatha he had just heard the news that Andrea had hanged herself in her cell. "If Henry had not been found, she could have got away with it," said Agatha. "Yes, we got that tape, but it's not admissible in court. A good barrister could probably have got her off. I suppose they didn't find anything in that room above the stables?"

"Not a thing. Damian has been charged with obstructing the police in their enquiries, harbouring a murderer and I forget what else," said Patrick. "But I'm sure a good lawyer will give him a get-out-of-jail-free card."

A week later, Agatha called at the vicarage. "I was about to call on you," said Mrs. Bloxby. "I haven't seen you in ages. You missed Gerald Devere's farewell party."

"I missed it because I wasn't invited and no one thought to tell me," said Agatha crossly.

"Now, that was very wrong of him. He invited the whole village. It was held in the church hall last week."

"So where has he gone?"

"Back to London."

"Glad to see it hasn't affected your new appearance," said Agatha, for the vicar's wife still had her hair tinted and was wearing a cheery red cashmere sweater.

"It all seems like a fevered dream," said Mrs. Bloxby. "How is Lord Charles?"

"Hasn't been near me. I think he sussed out I'd been to bed with Jake, and that is one one-night stand he is never ever going to forgive me for, and I don't know why."

"Perhaps he is beginning to care more for you than when you were just friends," suggested Mrs. Bloxby.

"I'm fed up all round," fretted Agatha. "No dramatic solving of the case. All just fizzled out, and any credit goes to Jake and the police. Do you know what the great detective has been doing today? Looking for a missing cat called Tiddles. Went round to the house. Looked up and there is the moggy on the roof."

"So you told the happy owner?"

"Well, no. I waited until the beast had climbed back down to the garden, nipped in, shoved it in a cat box and rang the bell. I'm sick of the type of animal lovers who think that animals are better than people any day because they want unconditional love without having to do much to earn it."

But as Agatha petted her cats when she got home, she said to them, "You don't give me unconditional love, do you? Your love is conditioned by the food I put in your furry mouths."

"So cynical." Charles's head rose above the sofa back, and he rubbed his eyes. "I was fast asleep."

Agatha experienced a spurt of sheer gladness. "Anything in particular bring you here?"

"Yes, come and sit down and I'll tell you. Get me a drink first. Whisky and soda."

When Agatha handed him the drink, he took a sip and said, "How would you like to come on holiday with me to Madeira?"

"Yes, I think so. Why Madeira?"

"That's where Jake was going, and it put the idea in my head."

"When?"

"Next week?"

"I don't know. Oh, what am I talking about? Of course I can get away."

"It's next Monday. Just for a week. The seven-twenty in the morning flight to Funchal. I'll meet you at Gatwick. Don't be late. I'm off home."

After he had left, Agatha experienced a warm glow. Not only was Charles back in her life, he was actually paying for a holiday for her.

To her amazement, she found they were flying business class. Charles was seated at the window, Agatha in the middle and a small child at the aisle with the child's parents in two seats opposite. "I tried to get us the two seats," muttered Charles, "but they were all booked up. You'd think the parents would want to sit with their brat."

During the flight, the child's parents passed over an iPad and said, "Watch *The Ruggies*."

Agatha remembered that *The Ruggies* was a children's television show about animated rugs. She was finding the squeaky voices of the animated rugs highly irritating when she suddenly heard a familiar voice saying, "Now then, bad ruggies. You mustn't quarrel." Agatha peered at the screen and saw Jake's face.

"I've just seen Jake," Agatha said to Charles. "He's on television."

"I read about that," said Charles. "He was head-hunted by an agent after that arrest he made and got the job on children's TV."

"Why didn't you tell me?"

"Because I don't want to talk about that piece of garbage. Right?"

Charles sounded unusually vehement, and Agatha began to feel sad. Charles must have been really keen on Olivia to resent Jake so much.

But when they arrived in mild warm sunshine, and she found they were to stay at the famous Reid's hotel, Agatha's spirits soared. They were given two rooms with a connecting door, and each had a sunny balcony overlooking the sea.

She opened the connecting door and shouted to Charles, "Going to have a shower."

"Right," he called back. "I'll see you in the bar."

Showered and changed into a cotton dress, Agatha was about to leave when she decided to have a look at Charles's room to see if it had the same view. It proved to be exactly the same. She was about to turn away when she saw a folder of papers with a travel agent's name on the bed.

She decided to have a quick look in case Charles had arranged a boat trip or something like that for them. A letter caught her eye. She wouldn't have read it had it not begun, "Dear Charles, I am so sorry . . ."

She sat down on the bed and proceeded to read it. It was from Olivia's father. Agatha's heart sank as she read it. It seemed that Jake was forgiven everything because of the television job and had said he was devoted to Olivia, so her father, thinking they could do with some time together, had bought them a week's holiday in Madeira. That was when Jake had moved out of Olivia's flat, found accommodation and refused to answer calls or messages. He ended by saying, "I feel you have suffered more than most of us from this wretched young man. So instead of cancelling the holiday, I am sending it all to you."

Agatha bit her lip in vexation. If Charles had told her the truth, she would not have hoped . . . But Agatha's mind clamped down on what she had perhaps hoped.

She went out and along the corridor to take the lift up to the bar. Reid's is built on a cliff, so you go down to the rooms.

The other occupant of the lift was a little old lady bent over two sticks.

"Life is a bitch," said Agatha and then blushed as she realised she had said it out loud.

"How very true," said the old lady.

Read on for an excerpt from

The Witches' Tree . . .

The next Agatha Raisin Mystery from M.C. Beaton,
available soon in hardcover from Minotaur Books!

The evening was not going well. The late Agatha
Christie would have been amazed to learn that
she was destined to be the ruin of some genteel dinner
parties. Otherwise intelligent people, after a move to a
village in the Cotswolds, can become keen to "do the
village thing," getting ideas of what it should be like
from her detective stories.

That was why Sir Edward Chumble and his wife,
Tiffany, had invited the vicar of St. Edmund in the
nearby village of Sumpton Harcourt and his wife to

dinner. "I mean, one is supposed to invite the vicar," said Tiffany.

The other guests were Tiffany's friend, Jane Oliver, an odd woman with a look of perpetual bad temper, an elderly judge, Lord Thurkettle, and two "bright young things," Brenda and Bengy Gentry who were in fact in their forties but chasing perpetual youth.

The vicar, Rory Harris, was not meek and scholarly. He was built like a rugby prop and had a deep commanding voice. His wife, Molly, was a truly glamorous redhead and that put Tiffany, who regarded herself as the fairest of them all, in a vicious temper.

The Chumbles had recently moved to the Cotswolds and Sir Edward was determined to play the role of squire. But no one touched their forelocks at his approach: in fact the locals seemed to find him a bit of a hoot. He had retired from the foreign office after a brief stint as ambassador in some former part of the Soviet Union that no one seemed to have heard of.

As ambassador, he had hoped to hold grand receptions in a palatial mansion, but the embassy was like a modern bungalow and the locals were insolent.

By moving to the Cotswolds, he fantasised of being head of a little fiefdom: gracious tennis parties, strawberries and cream and all that other lovely old England business. But the village, Cuckleton, although pretty enough, showed a marked lack of interest in the newcomers. To even be considered not worth gossiping about was a sad blow.

Tiffany recognised the dress Molly was wearing because she had seen it hanging up in a supermarket in Evesham, priced at a mere fifteen pounds. "So clever of you not to waste money on clothes, Molly," she cooed across the table. One of the talents necessary to being a good vicar's wife was the capacity to tell blatant lies.

"You mustn't tease me," said Molly. "You know this is Armani. I am just too shockingly expensive, amn't I darling?"

"Worth the money," boomed her husband. "Prettiest woman in the room."

Tiffany took another slug of carefully decanted South African hearty red and said, "So sorry. But darling, it does look like a Primark one I saw in Tesco's."

"Poor you," said Molly. "I wouldn't be seen dead in Tesco's. Of course, foreign offices' pensions must be too dire."

A maid hired for the evening came in with a trolley of coffee. Tiffany had hired her from a card on the post office bulletin board. The maid was called Mrs. Batterty and she looked to be in her nineties, which, in fact, she was, being ninety-five years old and creaking with arthritis. She was almost bent double. Pink scalp showed through her thinning white hair. Rory leapt to his feet to take coffee cups from her trembling hands.

When she had tottered from the room, Tiffany said, "I didn't know she was going to be so old, now did I?"

"That reminds me," said Molly, jumping to her feet. "We've left our darling with a sitter we don't know that well. Got to rush. Must excuse us."

"Didn't know you had a child," said Tiffany, escorting them to the front door and giving them each a limp hand to shake.

"We don't. It's our cat. Gets in a frightful state if we're away too long."

"I could kill that bitch," muttered Tiffany as she stalked back indoors. She confined herself to sweetly murdering the characters of the vicar and his wife. "So terribly sad," she told the remaining guests. "No children. Only to be expected. You see, the poor Church of England does attract closet gays, so they up and marry someone who will play along."

"But you haven't any children, sweetie, have you?" demanded Brenda Gentry. "Surely Edward isn't gay. Or was he shagging the peasants when you were out in God knows where? Joke! Don't bristle up. I'll have some more of your box wine."

"That is a fine vintage," boomed Sir Edward.

"But I went in to the kitchen to see if I could help and there was your missus decanting stuff out of a box of South African red into a decanter."

"She was leaving a drink for the servant," said

Edward desperately. "Good God! That the time? Sorry, folks. Long day. Must ask you to leave."

After the guests had left and his wife had gone to bed, Sir Edward remained at the table, brooding over the dirty dishes. Although he adored Agatha Christie detective stories, he saw himself more as Dorothy Sayers's Lord Peter Wimsey. He could feel one of his headaches coming on. How ghastly the Cotswolds had turned out to be. Perhaps it was because they had arrived at the dying end of the year. Come summer and surely he would be asked to open fetes. His eyes half closed as he went off into a dream of croquet on the lawn, cricket in the field, and strawberries and cream with everything.

"What a shit of an evening," said Molly who was driving. "I can hardly see in this bloody fog."

"You should have let me drive," said Rory.

"You wanted to drink, remember? Oh, why didn't you get a parish in Oxford or somewhere where there are lights and shops? Sumpton Harcourt is the arse-hole of the world."

Molly hunched over the steering wheel. A breeze started to move the fog which danced in swaying pillars in front of her headlights, somehow even more difficult to drive through than the previous thick fog. As she approached the village, through the shifting fog, she saw the lightning-blasted limbs of the witches' tree, as it was called.

"Look, Rory," said Molly. "Some idiot's dancing around in this . . ." She suddenly slammed on the brakes and screamed, "It's a body!"

Rory got a torch out of the glove compartment, hoping against hope some children had slung a dummy up on the branches. But the torch lit up the dead, contorted features of elderly Miss Margaret Darby, one of the church helpers. The vicar took out his mobile and then remembered that Sumpton Harcourt was one of those Cotswold villages which did not have a mobile phone signal. He went back to the car. "It's old Margaret Darby. Better phone from the vicarage."

"You go," said Molly. "I'd better climb up and make sure the poor thing is really dead."

It was at moments like these that Rory realised why he had married her.

He handed her the torch and ran off in the direction of the vicarage. Molly climbed up the branches and shone the torch into the swollen face. Fighting down a feeling of nausea, she stretched out a hand to the woman's neck and felt for a pulse. There wasn't even a flicker.

She retreated to the car. How had they failed the poor woman? She cleaned the brass in the church and arranged the flowers. She had seemed happy enough. If only she had asked for help.

Molly switched on the engine and turned on the heater. After a mere ten minutes Rory came running back. "Police and ambulance on their way."

He climbed in beside her and put an arm around her shoulders. "Did you have any idea she was suicidal?"

"No," said Molly. "We only exchanged platitudes. Things like, nasty weather. Isn't it cold?"

"It's pity they closed down all the village police stations," complained Rory. "Where do they have to come from now? Cheltenham? Mircester? Oh, I hear a siren."

A police car was the first to arrive. Only five minutes later, the ambulance arrived. A policeman donned a forensic suit, mask, gloves and boots and climbed up to examine the body. He shouted down to the paramedics that the body must be left where it was until a forensics team arrived.

"How awful," whispered Molly through white lips. "It seems indecent to leave the poor woman hanging there."

The companion of the policeman who had climbed up to examine the body came over to their car and took down their names and addresses. "Before you go any further," said Rory, "we've had a shock. You can find us at the vicarage round the next corner next to the church if you want statements."

"Very well, sir."

* * *

The vicarage was much as it had been under the tenancy of the previous vicar. It was dark and gloomy even on a sunny day because it was covered on the outside with ivy. There was no central heating and the floors were stone flagged. "Let's use my study," said Rory. "The fire's laid. I only need to strike a match."

The study did service as a living room because it had the one fire that did not smoke. It was dominated by a large desk with squat carved legs ending in griffins' heads. In front of the fire which Rory lit were two horsehair armchairs, slippery and uncomfortable. They kept meaning to replace them but ever since Rory had taken up his new post a month ago, there never seemed to be any time. He was also expected to preach at four other villages. Even Molly was kept busy with parish visits, and the various clubs held in the church hall: Women's Institute, Mothers' Union, Baking Night and Bible readings.

Like the Chumbles, they had been seduced by the thought of idyllic village life. Rory had been vicar of a parish in the East End of London. On a good Sunday, the congregation would amount to around twelve elderly people. On a bad one, much fewer as the church was invaded by drunken youths from the pub next door shouting insults. Tired of the hopelessness of trying to bring the word of God to people who did not want to hear it, tired of the squalor, horrified by a final attack they could not even bring themselves to talk about, they had been delighted at the chance to move to the beautiful Cotswolds. Also, there was a fairly large congregation on Sundays, people coming from neighbouring villages, attracted by the novelty of a handsome vicar . . .

They had seemed to live under constant threat in London and both were surprised to feel an undertone of fear in the village. Of course, the weather hadn't helped. Ever since they arrived, it had either been pouring rain or cold nights with thick fog. Then they were inclined to put it down to the village's Tudor buildings with their thatched roofs, crouched round the village green.

"I am so tired," said Molly, stifling a yawn. "And to think I believed that once we were in the Cotswolds all that I would have to do was to occasionally twitch the lace curtains. Rory!" She sat up straight. "Why wouldn't that policeman let the ambulance men cut her down?"

"You mean, was she murdered? No. Just routine. Like car accidents hold everything up on the motorway these days because of Health and Safety rules that say nothing to be shifted until the transport police and you name it have examined the wreckage."

"The villagers will have gathered to watch," said Molly. "Should I be out there with the tea urn?"

"No. They're probably having the time of their lives. You know, there's something ghoulish about them. That's the door. I'll get it."

Rory came back with two detectives who introduced themselves as Detective Sergeant Wong and Detective Constable Peterson. Wong looked half-Chinese and Peterson was a pretty woman with dark curly hair.

"Would you like some tea or coffee?" offered Molly. "Something stronger? Detective Peterson?"

"Oh, do call me Alice. I would love a cup of strong coffee and I am sure Bill here could do with one as well. I'll come and help you."

"I'll begin with you, sir," said Bill. "Where were you this evening?"

"We were at a dinner party at Sir Edward Chumble's in the next village, Cuckleton. We left about eleven o'clock. Molly was driving. The mist made it difficult to see anything.

"Then Molly and I saw the body in the headlights just as the fog shifted. There is no mobile phone signal here so I went back to the vicarage to call and Molly, my wife, climbed up to make sure the woman was really dead. Why did that policeman stop the ambulance men from bringing her down?"

"We have to wait for forensics when there is any death like this," said Bill. "So you left Sir Edward Chumble's home at, say, eleven o'clock. Are you sure of the time?"

"Oh, yes. It was a horrid dinner party and I kept looking at my watch and praying, 'Bring on the cheese! Oh, please, bring on the cheese.'"

"Who else was there?"

"Lady Edward, her aunt, a Jane Somebody, Lord Thurkettle and Brenda and Bengy Gentry."

"Were you the first to leave?"

"Yes. I hadn't met any of them before and it will be a cold day in hell before I want to meet any of them again."

"Why do you think you were invited?"

"The Cotswolds seem to be full of incomers all determined to do the village thing, you know, go to church at Easter and Christmas, invite the vicar and his wife, drive a four by four, wear green wellies and talk knowledgably about crops. Because my last parish was pretty rough, I did indulge in a bit of rural fantasy."

"Hang on until the spring comes," said Bill. "It becomes the prettiest place on earth."

Molly and Alice entered pushing an old creaking oak trolley laden with coffee cups, cafetiére and biscuits. Once coffee was served, Bill took Molly over her account. When she had finished, he said, "I'll save you a trip to police headquarters. I'll send someone tomorrow with your statements and get you to sign them."

"I believe the one traditional thing you do have in the Cotswolds is a Miss Marple," said Rory.

"Not that I know of," said Bill.

"But I read about her. Agatha Raisin! That's it."

Alice said, "Mrs. Raisin is not elderly, nor does she

knit. She is a private detective with offices in Mircester. She is rather attractive."

A picture of the policeman who had climbed the witches' tree came into Rory's head. He had been young and looked to be highly intelligent. "What's the name of that policeman who examined the body?" he asked.

"That would be PC Harold Turret." Bill would have liked to elaborate and say that Turret's nickname was Ferret. He not only worked extremely hard on cases but he also had a nasty habit of finding out everything he could about his fellows' private lives. Bill and Alice were secretly engaged because any liaisons between members of the force were frowned on. Unfortunately the Ferret showed every sign of being attracted to Alice.

"Are you sure," pursued Rory, "that it is suicide? She never seemed depressed or anything like that."

"We won't really know until the forensic team have put in their report. Good evening. Someone will call tomorrow with your statements."

When they had left, Molly said in a small voice, "Do you think we made a mistake coming here?"

"No," said her husband bracingly. "Wait till spring. People say it's marvellous then."

"Wouldn't it be awful if poor Miss Darby was murdered?" said Molly as they mounted the stairs.

"It wouldn't somehow," said Rory. "I feel guilty

about the idea of her being driven to suicide and us now knowing she was in such distress."

The bedroom was cold. It contained one of those mammoth Victorian wardrobes like the one in *The Chronicles of Narnia* and a four-poster bed, but without the hangings, Molly having torn them down.

"Are we going to bed in our muck?" asked Molly.

"You bet," said her husband, beginning to tear off his clothes. The bathroom was at the end of a long draughty corridor, and a monument to Victorian plumbing.

Molly sat down at the dressing table and began to remove her makeup with cosmetic wipes. Her face looked odd in the old glass, rather like some other Molly than a reflection.

"Hurry up!" called her husband. "I'm freezing!"

"That's all I am to you," said Molly. "A hot water bottle."

They had only been married a year but had planned to put off having children.

They decided, as they finally snuggled up together, not to have sex that night; decided by that odd marital telepathy that well-matched couples are lucky enough to have. Molly was just drifting off to sleep when a vivid picture of that body rose up in her mind. She could see it in the headlights, high up on the slippery branches of . . . "Rory! Wake up!"

"What! Who!"

"It's Margaret Darby."

"Oh, do go to sleep."

"Listen. The odd thing about Miss Darby was that she always wore high heels. Not stilettos but not kitten heels either. She still had them on!"

"So?"

"They didn't have any straps. They were patent leather pumps. She was high up in the slippery branches and the branches were gleaming with wet. She couldn't possibly have climbed up in those shoes."

"There's a song about that," mumbled Rory sleepily, "something like 'What? In these shoes?'"

"But Rory . . ."

"Look, if she's been murdered, the police will find out who did it. That is not our job. Don't interfere."

And neither the vicar nor his wife would have dreamt for a moment of interfering in police work had it not been for the fact that their statements were brought to them the next day by Police Constable Turret. Molly thought he had a clever interesting face, although critics might find something ratlike about it. He had small brown eyes.

After they had signed their statements, he asked, "Any chance of a cup of coffee, love?"

"If you are talking to me," said Molly, frost in her voice, "ask properly."

"Oh, Gawd!" said Turret, giving what he fancied as a jolly laugh. "One of them women libbers, hey!"

Molly shrugged, suddenly wanting him to go, but she left the room to fetch coffee.

"Have you anything to ask me or are you waiting to patronise my wife again?" asked Rory.

"Sorry about that," said Turret, making a mental note to make the vicar's life miserable in some way. "Now, you and the missus are like the first suspects."

"Like how?" demanded Rory. "Twenty minutes before we found the body we were taking our leave of Sir Edward. We've signed our statements to that effect." He got to his feet to open the door for Molly because he had heard the creaking approach of the old trolley.

"I had it all ready in the hope that nice detective would come back," said Molly.

Turret leapt to his feet. "Can I help, gorgeous?"

Rory said evenly, "We can help ourselves. Molly, why don't you find out if Miss Darby had any relatives?"

"Good idea," said Molly, thankful of the chance to escape. It wasn't Turret's comments that upset her: it was the way his eyes seemed to crawl over her body, and, yes, there was something frightening about him. She decided to go over to Carsely and call on the vicar's wife there, Sarah Bloxby. Sarah seemed to know about everyone for miles around and might know the dead Margaret's relatives.

As soon as she drove out of Sumpton Harcourt she could feel a weight of anxiety lift from her shoulders. The day was dark and misty and drenched fields stretched from side to side.

To her disappointment, when she was ushered into the vicarage drawing room in Carsely she found another visitor there, a fashionably dressed woman with a good figure, long legs and small bearlike eyes.

Mrs. Bloxby performed the introductions. She served coffee and said, "It must have been very upsetting for you, finding the body."

"I wish someone would upset me with a dead body," grumbled her other visitor. "I've got nothing but lost cats and divorces on the books."

"Oh, you're that Agatha Raisin," exclaimed Molly. "You know, if we had the money, I would be tempted to employ you."

"Perhaps Mrs. Raisin might be interested in a few facts," said Mrs. Bloxby.

Agatha laughed. "Mrs. Bloxby knows I am always interested in dead bodies."

"You use second names?" asked Molly.

"A bad habit," said Agatha, "developed when we had a genteel Ladies' Society here. It's hard to break."

Molly leaned her back against the feathered cushions on the old sofa and told them about the dinner party and how they had found the body. The wood fire crackled on the hearth and from outside came the sweet sound of the tenor bell in the church tower. "The wind must have got up," said Mrs. Bloxby.

At first Molly talked about the dinner party and then how she had found the body. She went on to describe the two detectives and then the visit from Turret. Suddenly, she found herself crying and hiccupping and gasping out how horrible the vicarage was and how beastly the bloody Cotswolds had turned out to be. A box of tissues was placed on her lap and Mrs. Bloxby's quiet voice said, "Drink this." Molly dried her eyes and took a gulp. It was sweet and warming. "What is this?" she asked.

"It's dandelion wine," said Mrs. Bloxby. "Early in the day for alcohol but it contains a lot of sugar."

"I don't know what came over me," said Molly. "I'm pretty tough. It's the village. It's creepy."

"That vicarage is pretty awful," said Mrs. Bloxby. "So big and nothing changed since Queen Victoria. I'll drive over and see if I can do something to help."

"We'll go now," said Agatha. "Saturday, and not even a date."

How old was she? Molly began to worry. This Raisin

woman was middle-aged but she carried an aura of sensuality. The trouble with being a vicar's wife was one often had to deal with women getting crushes on your husband. So far, not one had been anything to worry about, but Agatha Raisin might be another matter.